Dark Vortex

Dark Vortex

Mated by Magic

Stella Marie Alden, Chantel Seabrook

Copyright (C) 2016 Stella Marie Alden, Chantel Seabrook
Layout design and Copyright (C) 2016 Creativia
Published 2016 by Creativia
ISBN: 978-1540574831
Cover art by Virginie Wernert – www.designedbyqueenninie.com
This book is a work of fiction. Names, characters, places, and incidents are the product of the author's imagination or are used fictitiously. Any resemblance to actual events, locales, or persons, living or dead, is purely coincidental.
All rights reserved. No part of this book may be reproduced or transmitted in any form or by any means, electronic or mechanical, including photocopying, recording, or by any information storage and retrieval system, without the author's permission.
stellamariealden@gmail.com
chantelseabrook@gmail.com

Chapter 1

The door chimes clanged and two large men, carrying a third, burst into the tea shop.

Zoe jumped up and her fresh coffee toppled onto her lap. *Hot. Hot. Hot.*

"Where's Olivia? We need her. *Now.*" The older of the two strangers ignored her dance of pain and struggled with the weight of the man he carried.

"I aah..." She pushed her glasses up her nose, shaking out her wet shorts, and pointed to the curtain. "Put him on the daybed in the backroom."

She grabbed her cell phone, and tapped her cousin's number.

Five... six... unanswered rings. *Come on Liv, pick up.*

"Help us," the younger man yelled from the doorway.

With an uneven breath, she left the ice cream parlor décor of the front room and entered the exam room. Even before she approached the men, the overpowering stench of rotting fish made her stomach turn. She swallowed the bile that rose in her throat.

"You're both going to have to leave." The two glared, refusing to budge, and she gritted her teeth. "I can't help him with you close by."

She pointed to the paisley curtain that divided the two spaces.

The men snarled, but obeyed. When they were gone, she took a deep breath and tried her cousin again. *Please pick up.*

"Hi, leave a message for Olivia's Natural Herbal Remedies..." *Damn, damn, damn.*

The man on the bed moaned and Zoe took a tentative step toward him. His white t-shirt was torn, the fabric charred at the edges, but his olive skin seemed unscathed. He needed a doctor, not an herbal concoction. The people in this town were even crazier than the ones she'd encountered during her short stay in New York.

She should call his friends back and tell them, or better yet, dial 911. Zoe was about to do just that when she saw it. *What the hell?*

Under the man's skin, a leach-like creature strained and writhed, making black web marks. She swallowed a scream and backed into the large cabinet where Olivia kept her herbs and tonics. She'd seen a lot of weird shit over the past three months, since coming to stay with her cousin, but this had to be the craziest.

Zoe glanced at her phone and cursed Olivia for leaving her alone. She didn't know how to deal with this voodoo crap. Liv was the self-proclaimed healer. No matter how many times her cousin had tried to teach her to read auras and understand herbology, Zoe couldn't wrap her brain around it.

What would Liv do if she were here? Probably chant some ritual prayer and make tea.

"Tea–" She could do that. Keeping a close watch on him, she put the kettle on to boil.

The man had gone still, his skin stark white in comparison to the inky lines that sketched over face, down his neck, arms, and chest. Zoe shivered. She took a few tentative steps towards the bed and knelt beside him.

She moved his matted bangs, and placed her palm to his forehead. He was burning up, but at least he was still alive.

"Where's Liv?" Large fingers clamped around her forearm.

The black substance seemed to enter her from where he held her in his vise-like grip, and her stomach twisted and cramped. Little pinpricks of light floated before her eyes, and something else, something much more intimate, mixed with the dark energy.

For a moment, time seemed to stand still. Ice and fire rushed through her, down her arms and legs, to the tips of her fingers and toes. A strange wind rushed through the room, causing her dark hair to whip around her face.

The kettle screamed for her attention. She flinched, but he didn't release her. His nostrils flared and his pupils dilated.

The man was handsome, if you ignored the slight crook in his once broken nose. The dark stubble on his chin and upper lip outlined high cheekbones, square jaw, and full lips. But it was the eyes that caught her attention, the lightest brown, with flecks of gold that seemed to flicker in the dim light.

"Who are you?" he growled between clenched teeth.

The energy between them increased until Zoe was certain the entire room would combust into flames. Fear overpowered the desire that swelled within her.

"Let me go." The words caught in her throat and came out as a strangled cry.

He uncurled his fingers and thumped his head back on the daybed, groaning.

Zoe staggered back to Liv's workstation and placed her hands on the counter. With steadying breaths, she prepared the tea the way she'd seen Liv do it a hundred times. She just prayed that she was using the right ingredients. There wasn't anything in any of the tins that could make him worse than he already was–*she hoped.*

The man let out a roar of pain, and gripped the edge of the bed as his body seized and stiffened. The poison seemed to be expanding, tearing through his body like a predator consuming its prey.

She was close to panicking. No, she was already panicking. This was too much. She didn't have the skill or the knowledge needed to help him. She could barely read a damn aura.

Olivia would know what to do, but her cousin wasn't answering her fricking phone.

With trembling fingers, Zoe held his head and forced the hot liquid down his throat. After a gulp, he turned and puked out a black, rancid mass.

Zoe dropped the cup and scooted backwards, the meager contents of her own stomach burning her esophagus. This was not what she signed up for when she accepted her cousin's proposal to come stay with her. Hell, she hadn't even known the woman existed until a few months ago. Liv was strange on the best of days, with her New Age ideas, and bizarre beliefs in the paranormal. But until today, her outlandish stories of healers and warriors had just been that–stories.

The man seized again, then went still. His forehead was damp with perspiration, his skin still streaked with black webs. The putrid smell of impending death lingered around him. A chill went up and down Zoe's spine. She didn't know how she knew the scent, but the knowledge seeped through her like an old memory.

"No. You are not going to die." She threw open the cupboard doors. A vast collection of colorful tins lined the shelves. *Ugh.* Licorice, sassafras, and dried mold. She glowered, compelling their auras forth, like Liv had taught her, but only shades of brown danced in front of her eyes.

He was going to die because she couldn't find the right fucking tea.

"Dammit!" She slammed the door and it banged.

A rattling sound came from the man's chest. She'd never felt so helpless in her life.

You know what to do. The words pierced her mind, sending a zing through her body. She closed her eyes and a flash of memory infused her. It was hazy, but there was power and knowledge in the vision.

The room started to spin and she had to grasp the counter to keep from falling.

You know what to do. The words echoed like a soft hum within her.

The man would die if she did nothing.

With a sharp intake of breath, she focused on the words that raced through her mind and drew from the strange energy that vibrated around her. She didn't have time to think about how crazy the entire situation was. She just knew she had to save him. At her beckon, a small wind formed in her palms, then blew across the room, and entered the man.

The color drained from his face, his eyes went wide, and he inhaled sharply.

Zoe refocused and tried again. This time the lights flickered and a deep purple cloud materialized for a moment before disappearing. If she wasn't so focused on saving him, she would have been terrified.

She closed her eyes, centered like she'd learned in yoga class, and added a short prayer to the Goddess of Life. *Help me save him.*

Perhaps the prayer clinched the deal. The power within started with a buzzing in her ears. It bubbled up and surrounded her like an electric current. When she could no longer endure the pain, she screamed and fell back onto the wood floor.

She'd fired a shotgun once, but this discharge had a hell-of-a worse kick. A black-violet cloud of energy sizzled and snapped above her head in a wild frenzy. When it didn't move, Zoe willed it forward to kill the poison in the man.

Suddenly, the conjured plasma zoomed around the exam room and lit seven colored candles. It went into the cupboards and rattled the tin cans until two fell off the top shelf with a clunk. The energy morphed and twisted into a sparkling tornado, hovered momentarily above the man's bed, and disappeared into his body. Zoe was unable to breathe again until it reappeared with a dark shadow caught up in its spin.

Chapter 2

Jack reached for his chest, expecting to feel a sticky pool of blood, but his hand came back dry. That vortex had knifed right through him, yet he was still alive.

"It's not done." The healer pointed above his head where the spinning energy still hovered.

She tried to stand, but fell forward on her hands and knees, breathing heavily. She scrambled crab-like towards the tins on the floor, tried to wobble up the cabinets, but slipped back. Her head hit the floor with a thud and she stopped moving.

Jack staggered off the daybed, checked her pulse. It was weak, but she was still breathing. Something stirred inside him at the touch, but he was too drained to analyze it.

He hobbled to the kitchenette and grabbed the ancient tins. The steaming water from the kettle made a too-hot concoction, reeking of sweaty sneakers. After a quick gag and gulp, the menacing cloud dissolved through the walls with an anticlimactic sizzle and pop.

"What the hell was that?" He'd been to healers more times than he'd like to recall, but this beat all. He squatted over the unconscious woman.

The front door opened and a cool breeze blew at the curtain.

"What did you do to Zoe?" Olivia stormed into the room, followed by Stan and Luke. Her red hair flew behind her in a mass of tangled curls.

"She's alive." Weak-kneed, Jack stood, and leaned against a wall.

Olivia ordered Luke to carry the woman to the daybed. The younger man obeyed, his face skewed in a snarl.

"Thought we lost you out there." Stan looked him over, smiled and slapped him on the back, his eyes moist with unshed tears.

Jack nodded. He had to admit, that was *way* too close.

Olivia pursed her lips and placed her hand on the woman's forehead.

"Is she okay?" Jack asked, rubbing his chest.

"Aura's fairly normal...for her...but she's suffering deep exhaustion from an extreme energy burn."

He took a step forward and staggered. Stan caught him by the elbow, steadying him.

"Sit down before you break something," Olivia ordered, pointing at a chair. She crossed the room and placed a cool palm on Jack's cheek. A familiar pulse of energy coursed through him. As she read his health, her eyes went wide, and then narrowed. "What went on here?"

"Let's just say she has a very unusual healing technique, and she cut it way too close." He was still reeling from the effects of the energy blast, followed by the vortex, and the foul tasting tea. There was something else he needed to remember, but couldn't put his finger on it. *Shit, what was it?*

Olivia eyed him a bit more closely and glared like a first grade teacher. "I'm not sure what just happened in here but

I can sure as hell tell it wasn't good. When I agreed to take care of your clan, you assured me it was for easygoing solstice quarrels. I thought you guys were above this level of stupidity. Didn't we both agree that dueling was archaic?"

His eyes narrowed at her tone. "It *is* archaic! Tonight, I saved Luke from an underage witch-ling. She was out trolling for a mate and she hooked him. When I tried to separate the two, he gave me one minor, albeit painful, shot."

He glared at Luke who shrugged and glanced at the floor.

"Then, while I was catching my breath, someone tried to assassinate me. I never even saw it coming." Jack shook his head, then winced at the pain the action sent shooting through his skull. "It was a hell of a night. Worst ever. God, I hate solstice."

"Did you recognize who did it?" Olivia's brows furrowed.

"Didn't see him." Jack scrubbed his fingers over his face. "Never felt that kind of power before."

She frowned, put both hands to his chest, and closed her eyes. Her healing energy hit him like a good night's sleep followed by jolt of strong coffee.

He sucked in every bit she offered.

Straitening, she put her hands on her hips.

"Your assistant did an oddly adept job of healing me, then collapsed and banged her head." He snuck a look at the woman on the bed. "Are you sure she's okay?"

Olivia glanced over briefly, then back at him. "She'll be fine."

"Good." There was something about her that piqued his interest.

"What aren't you telling me?" Olivia cocked her head and waited for the truth, which he had no intention of giving.

He'd never seen a vortex before, let alone one with healing powers.

"What?" He feigned his most innocent look.

"Zoe hasn't shown *any* knack for healing." Liv shook her head. "No matter. I'll get the truth out of *you*, later." She turned to Stan and Luke and covered her nose. "Whatever hit Jack caused an evil aura mess and the stink has rubbed off on you. I'll blend some tea and bring it down to the beach. The ocean breeze should clean up the rest."

"But we were just out there and it's cold." Luke whined more like the kid Jack remembered than the eighteen-year-old he'd just saved from a greedy teenage paranormal.

Jack snorted. "Don't argue with Olivia or she'll conjure up something that will make you sorry you did. Besides, you probably still need a little cooling off."

Stan mumbled something about snotty healers as they headed out the door. Olivia shut it firmly behind them and the bells on the door clanged as if in agreement.

"There's something very off with Stan's aura." Her brows drew down in a deep frown. "Keep an eye on him for the next couple days."

Jack grunted at her vague warning.

Olivia continued to mutter to herself as she prepared the tea, but he tuned her out, turning his attention to the strange woman. He was close enough to see the small goosebumps on her bare arms and legs–she was cold.

Guilt crept over him. She had saved his life, and now she was suffering for it. He stood, his legs sturdier than before, and picked up the quilt at the end of the bed. Leaning down, he placed it over her legs and caught her scent. Strawberries and... *It couldn't be.* He sniffed again and froze.

Jack breathed her in and blood rushed to his groin. Memories of years of searching flashed through his mind. The trips overseas. The despair, the resignation, and the final blow. Settling for a love-match with that heart breaker, Diane.

He brushed his fingers over her cheek and an erotic buzz coursed through his body. *Holy shit.* His balls tightened painfully and his cock hardened in demand. Every muscle in his body went tense, and his gut clenched with soul shattering desire.

She was the one.

His mate.

He all but sank to his knees in prayerful thanksgiving.

Olivia must have caught the flare in his aura because she coughed roughly behind him. She gave him an evil eye, which would've gotten her stoned to death a hundred years ago.

"Don't even think about it." She pointed a finger at him. "She's a minimally talented healer at best, not a warrior. Mating with her won't work."

He shook his head and almost contradicted her. Zoe wasn't from the healer clan. She was a strong warring talent. And yet she'd healed him. *Impossible.* That was the thread he was trying to remember.

Good God.

The sleeping Zoe was one badass warring witch with powers that had to match his own or he wouldn't feel this irresistible urge to mate.

But Olivia was never wrong.

Maybe the deathblow had affected his reason. He swallowed hard. "That reminds me. Our deal was that you would keep the shop open during the nights of solstice. Where were you tonight?"

"I *was* open." Olivia went back to sniffing at teas, holding them up in the air. Seeing things he couldn't.

"Well, in the future try to keep your cell phone on. That's what your retainer is for."

"When I got Stan's message, I rushed back as fast as I could." Her eyes narrowed. "By the way, just how did Zoe find the herbs to heal you? I thought she was aura colorblind."

"Dunno. I was out cold. Ask her when she wakes up." What else could he say? Jack Fialko, leader of the Iesco clan, was rendered stupid?

He slid over to his solstice choice, took Zoe's hand, and tried to reach into her sleeping mind. Olivia just had to be wrong. Years of looking and he'd never before craved a woman–not like this. He gently removed her glasses and was surprised to see a beautiful eastern European face hiding behind the thick lenses. His cock took more interest than he'd thought possible.

"I'm staying here tonight. Too tired to leave. I'll take the small spare room." He wasn't taking any chances that the woman would escape.

"That's not part of our deal." She placed a cup of tea on the table and motioned him to sit. "It's going to take me a week to get the stinking darkness out of here as it is."

"It's not up for discussion. I'm staying." He gave her a lopsided grin and sat down at the table. "Least you can do for almost letting me die."

Olivia put a hand to Zoe's forehead and frowned.

"I don't like this. Why don't you give my tea a minute to douse that lust of yours? She can't be a match." Under her breath she said, "At least I don't think so."

"You know something?" Jack tore off the edges of three sugar packs at once and raised an eyebrow.

"To be honest, I can't quite read her aura." Olivia shook her head, causing her dark red curls to bounce around her pixie-like face. "I'm missing something critical. I'll be damned if I know what it is."

"What about her parents?"

"Never met them. Apparently, they died when she was little. She was put up for adoption. Raised by humans. I still don't think she really believes in any of this."

"Shit," Jack muttered. That could complicate things. But if she was truly untrained, then how had she produced the vortex?

"I'll be back in a few. I meant what I said." Olivia gave him her best don't-screw-up face. "She's not one of your witches to be fucked and discarded."

Jack winced. She was right about one thing, this Zoe wasn't a woman to be discarded. She was, however, a woman to fuck. And he had every intention of doing so.

Carrying two mugs of tea, Olivia disappeared through the door. Mist and wind rushed in, the ocean crashed, and doorbells clanged. Then, all was quiet.

Alone at last. Jack sat down on the bed and brushed the dark hair off Zoe's forehead. For the first time in years, he allowed himself to imagine what it might be like to pass on his powerful genes to children. To know his clan would be safe for another generation.

Her lashes fluttered open, and her brows drew down when her eyes focused on him.

"You're okay?" she whispered.

"Oh, no. I'm definitely not *okay*, Zoe." He let the Z linger across his tongue. He breathed in her exotic scent and cupped her cheek in one hand. Oh man. She got to him.

"What? Is the darkness back? Is Olivia here?" She reached blindly over the driftwood side-table and on the floor beside the bed. "Where're my glasses?"

"No. It's not the darkness." His hands shook when he placed her glasses on her nose. Her big brown eyes focused on him behind the thick lenses. Overwhelmed, he choked out the words he'd longed to say for years. "I want you for my mate."

"What?" Her eyes went huge. She shuffled to a sitting position with her back pressed tightly against the headboard.

Holy Goddess. Her body said yes and her mouth said no. Olivia had to be wrong. Zoe was perfectly trained for the ritual about to unfold.

He placed his hand on her bare thigh, just below where her shorts ended, and allowed his heat and energy to infuse her. She squirmed, pulling her legs together. *So nice. So sweet.* He added tiny jolts of electricity as he stroked her bare leg, and chuckled at her responsiveness. Her full lips parted, and her gaze went to his mouth.

Not yet, Angel.

"I've been looking for you for a lifetime." He touched a lock of her dark hair. "You're my hope. My salvation."

"I can't be." Her soft breath hit his nostrils with a scent that spoke of sex.

His brothers had warned him about the hot and the cold of the mating ritual, but how could anyone truly be prepared?

"You're not already mated?" He held his breath.

She shook her head and her lips parted.

He exhaled. "You'll be mine, now. Forever."

Reaching out, he gently pulled the elastic from her hair, and the long, dark locks fell over her shoulders. She closed her eyes and moaned. He moved closer, caressing her cheek, inhaling her intoxicating scent. *Strawberries and beach sand.* His cock swelled.

She whimpered.

His tongue glued to the roof of his mouth. Never had he imagined that his clan's sacred oath would be so hard to say.

"Fight me off, witch."

Her eyes went wide and then she dissed him with a flawless amount of disdain. "I am not a witch."

He laughed. Her act couldn't be any better.

She placed her hands on his chest and gave him a small shove. "Listen, what's your name? Jack? You're very…attractive…but this is *so* not going to happen."

"You know how this works. Either fight me off or kiss me. Decide." There wasn't a whole lot of rational thought left in Jack's mating-brain.

"Okay. I choose to fight." She scrunched up her face, raised her arm, and screamed. A violet vortex zoomed out of her hand and hit him dead center in the chest.

He was thrown clear across the room and lay on the floor with his eyes closed. Her sweet, beautiful energy exploded into his torso. Her essence was laced with stars, ocean breeze, and a silver moon. God almighty, he was so hard that he wasn't sure if he'd last another minute.

"I knew you wanted me! Stop messing with me." He needed to get the pressure off his dick. He unfastened his jeans, pulled his t-shirt over his head, and opened his arms wide. "Go ahead. Throw everything you have at me."

"Dammit. What part of *no* are you not getting?" Her mouth curled down and she scooted into a corner of the daybed, as far away from him as possible.

Was that fear he saw in her eyes?

Something was off. He'd heard all the stories of mating from his brothers, friends, and even his father. Every woman was different, but at some point, they turned as lusty as the male. But fear was never a part of it. What was going on? He'd give her anything she asked to feel that vortex rock his balls again.

He crossed the room and tried a different tact. "Give me your hand."

She slid further into the corner, but after a moment, she held out a tentative hand.

The hair on his arms stood on end as he gathered all the spare electrons in the room to him. He laced the energy with his fierce lust, his dreams, his everything. He put his whole heart out on the line as far as it would go. This moment was the most important one of his entire life and he wasn't going to blow it. He gave her it all.

Her eyes went round, her legs fell open, and her head fell back. She panted and gasped for breath. He forced another surge of erotic energy into her body and a keening wail tore from her throat.

He smiled at the lust that infused her eyes. "You want more?"

She nodded hesitantly, biting her lip.

Thank fucking God. He pulled her down on the bed, under him. Through her thin shorts, he could feel her wet heat against his bare waist. The air sizzled around them. Desire, a living, breathing entity that pushed him close to the edge.

She was trembling, shaking against him. Her mouth opened in invitation. It was all he needed. He covered her lips with his, and the whole world exploded. His fingers clenched in her hair, and he tasted her. Sweet, perfection.

His brain was dazed with the overload of sensations. It was so fucking good, but not enough.

Barely able to pull away, he rasped, "What are you waiting for, angel? Fill me with your energy. Fight me."

Her brows creased. "Fight you? I thought you said you wanted me."

"I do." He gritted his teeth and pushed himself off the bed. *What game was she playing?* "But not like this."

"I don't understand." Her lips trembled.

Why wouldn't she fight him?

She tucked her hair behind her ears. Her eyes wide, innocent, and yet filled with cock-swelling lust.

He moved quickly, boxing her against the wall, his palms firmly planted beside her head.

"Stop playing around and fight me." He counted the awful seconds that felt like eternity.

"What the hell?" Anger glittered in her eyes and flushed her face. "You said kiss you or fight you off. I kissed you."

"You're serious, aren't you? You really don't know?" He gave a hard shake of his head and stared back at her incredulously. The tips of Jack's ears throbbed and his gut wrenched. He'd tried cocaine once as a teenager. His heart had raced, his hands had shook, and he'd wondered how the hell to get more… and then more. This was so much worse.

He took a fist and hit the drywall beside the bed, creating a gaping hole. The pain in his hand eased the one clutching at his gut.

Her eyes widened and her mouth gaped open, tears swelling in her eyes.

Great. Can I fuck this up any worse?

"Dammit all to hell." He wiped his hands over his face and fought for control. "You're not a healer. That vortex is a warrior trait. It's for fighting enemies, not curing headaches."

"What?" Her voice squeaked up an octave.

"Know how long I've been looking for you? Ten years. Ten fucking long years and I finally find you and you're clueless. I could've killed you. You could've killed me. I need to get out of here before I do something stupid and try to start this up again."

Jack tore out the front door and let his cursing bring up a fierce storm. He stayed on the beach until the frigid pelts of water doused his raging lust.

Chapter 3

Zoe rubbed her palms over her arms and legs and briefly closed her eyes. What had just happened? Her body was still vibrating from the pleasure of the man's touch. Never had she felt anything like the raging desire he stirred in her. It was just her luck that the man was stark, raving mad. She pulled the pillow over her face and groaned into it.

Olivia came back into the shop and raised a brow at her. "You're awake."

"Yeah." Zoe tried to adjust her hair and clothes but it was obvious she was sex-mussed. Humiliation mixed with her confusion and she let out a rough sigh.

"I just saw Jack down on the beach with his family." Olivia deposited the empty mugs she carried into the sink, then turned and leaned against the counter, arms crossed over her chest. "I don't think I've ever seen him angrier. What happened?"

"Oh, Liv. I don't even know." She threw her hands up. "I know I'm not privy to all your weird shit, but I'm really at a serious disadvantage here. What the hell's going on?"

Olivia nodded at the new hole in the wall. "You didn't by any chance throw some kind of energy into him?"

"I guess." She looked down at her hands and cringed, remembering. Her voice was weak when she spoke again, "I blasted him, but that was before he punched the wall."

Olivia frowned, pursed her lips, and narrowed her gaze. "Exactly what was his reaction when you...blasted him?"

"He laughed." Zoe put her legs to her chest and thumped her forehead against her knees. If she hadn't needed a therapist before, she definitely needed one now. The thought of driving the short distance from the Jersey Shore to New York to visit Dr. Larry seemed like a reasonable option.

"And... did he do the same thing to you?" Olivia sat down next to her and put out her hand to stop the head-banging. "Blast you with energy?"

"No. I mean...he just touched my hand and I went all ga-ga. His touch went straight between my thighs. I've never been that into a guy before, let alone ready to tear his clothes off." She covered her face with her hands and moaned. "He said I was his freaking mate."

"Oh shit," Olivia muttered, standing abruptly. "We've got to talk. But first, I need to cleanse the shop. Give me a few minutes. The aura in here is all fucked up."

It was more than the aura in the room that was fucked up. Zoe clamped her lips and kept that thought to herself.

Olivia pulled out a huge crock-pot shaped like a big black cauldron and started throwing herbs and spices into in it. It dwarfed the small stove. Occasionally she glanced up at Zoe and frowned.

Could the day get any weirder?

"While I'm cleaning, read this." Olivia placed a book the size of a medieval bible on the tiny tea table. Dust flew up from it and clogged the air.

"Seriously?" Zoe stood and eyed the huge book.

"Seriously," Olivia said with a stern nod. "You're in deep shit and you better know what you're in for. How the hell did I miss you having a strong warring talent? I don't even want to speculate on what that means."

Zoe sat down and opened the musty smelling book, titled 'Witches of the Warring Clan.'

"Liv, I've told you. I'm not into this witchcraft stuff. It freaks me out."

Olivia shook her head and went back to her pot. "Just read."

Zoe flipped the pages and started reading. The book was filled with outlandish tales of ancient lore. It had *The Hobbit* beat by a long shot.

Hours passed before Zoe finally pushed her chair back, stood, and stretched her sleeping muscles.

Olivia chanted while adding peppermint and anise to a blackened iron pot.

Brownies baked in one oven and chocolate chip cookies in another. The whole house smelled of yumminess.

"There's no dark aura in the world that can compete with this." Olivia grabbed a hot mitt, and removed the steaming confection from the oven rack.

Olivia sliced two hot gooey squares, gingerly put them in bowls, and scooped vanilla ice cream over the top. Two perfect volcanoes. Sweet creamy lava spread over the chocolate landscape.

After a couple bites, Zoe almost felt normal.

If nothing else, tonight she'd learned her libido wasn't broken after all. The man she'd healed gave her panty-twisting, breast-aching, gotta-have-him lust. But that didn't mean he was her mate, or that she was somehow from some warring clan.

"Oh heavenly Goddess, we'll have to work out for days for this sinful calorie intake," Olivia said, in between mouthfuls.

"But it's so worth it." Zoe smiled, then frowned when she remembered something she'd read. She still didn't know what to believe, but she couldn't help but be curious. "The book mentioned a perfect match. Do you know anything about it?"

"Most likely a myth." Olivia shrugged. "The talents of two witches combine when they mate, making both more powerful. The closer the match, the more power is shared. A perfect match would result in complete harmony of power. I've never seen it happen but Jack swears he has."

"Huh? Dumb it down for me. They only marry some perfect-match-y person?"

"No. Witches can choose to marry anybody..."

"But?"

"During solstice, something happens in their DNA. They crave to find a match. A perfect match is best. I guess evolution created a survival mechanism. A way to keep from diluting their powers over the centuries."

The hairs on the back of Zoe's neck and arms stood on end as if electricity had suddenly shot through her body.

"Who is the clan warring with?" Zoe asked, changing the subject. "Doesn't say anything about that in the book."

"They don't war with anyone anymore. They've signed treaties with most of the other clans."

"Then why call them warring?"

"The term is centuries old." Olivia shrugged and licked her spoon. "Let's just say they have a tendency to fight for what they want."

"And the men, tonight. They're part of this...warring clan?"

"They're Iesco. The most powerful clan on the east coast." Olivia's face went tight. "Jack's their leader."

Zoe shivered and heat spread through her limbs at the mention of the man's name.

"So, what powers do they use? To fight with, I mean."

"Warring witches capture the electrons around them. They can focus them on a target. Most can only generate a mild electric current."

"Can you?"

"Definitely not." Olivia shook her head. "Healers see auras and sense people's illnesses. We use that knowledge to heal. I've already shown you just about everything I can do."

"So what about my tornado thingy?"

Olivia paused mid-bite and stared open-mouthed at her. "You conjured a vortex? I've never seen anything stronger than what Jack's family doles out. I thought the rest pure myth."

This time when Zoe shivered, it was fear that sent a chill down her spine. She still didn't want to believe that any of this was real, but how could she doubt what she'd seen with her own eyes?

Chapter 4

Two months prior

Ivar smiled to himself and hummed a Russian folk tune. Perhaps in a day or so, he would call his clan leader in Moscow and let him know of his progress. Perhaps not. Soon he would not have to beg and bow to that pompous ass.

He had located his target again. The woman had left New York and found a nest of American relatives in southern New Jersey. The task of taking the witch home was going to be a bit trickier. The woman remained under the curse his healer had placed on her, still unable to use her powers, but she was smarter than he'd given her credit for.

"Tupa Shmara," he cursed. *Woman witches.*

The world would be better if they could keep them strapped to a gurney with their legs open wide, ready to take in sperm, and spit out babies. As he pictured that pleasant thought, he opened his computer and began to check the progress of the rest of his plan.

Most of his young drug mules were in Europe being prepped for a wonderful trip to the US, courtesy of a small Baptist church in Pennsylvania. *Do-gooders! Ha!* Ivar chuckled. How horrified would those little old women and milk-toast men be to know he'd stuffed those Afghani girls full of grade 'A' heroin?

He made a mental note to tell the girls again what would happen to their families if they tried to speak a word to anyone. After their very holy retreat, he would decide which ones to sell as prostitutes, and which to use again. It was all a matter of profitability and that's what kept his clan alive.

Some of the poppy growers in Afghanistan were quite desperate when he'd called in their debts. Was it his fault the farmers had let the Americans burn their fields? They were lucky that his clan had allowed them to pay their debt with daughters instead of death.

"Uncle Ivar?" A girl stood by the door holding a tray of food. Her dark hair was pulled back in a ponytail, making her look younger than her thirteen years.

He needed to find a buyer for that one before his cousin found out. He'd no idea how she happened into the group of mules, nor did he care. He was not one to check the teeth of a horse that fate had bestowed upon him.

"Erina, come in." Ivar stopped what he was doing and spoke to the girl in her native tongue, ushering her forward. He took the food, then patted her on the head. She gave him a dimpled smile before scurrying off in the direction she came from.

Ignorant fool, he thought, shoving a kalduny in his mouth and turning back to the computer.

But why would she not trust him? Hadn't he fed her well, and given her new American jeans to wear? Soon her body would be full and ripe for the taking, and he would find a needy witch to take her off his hands. If he could be patient, he might wait for a few years, until she reached puberty, to see what level power she possessed.

Ivar picked up his phone and dialed the New Jersey number. It was pure luck that he had contacts so close to where his target had taken up residence. He could, as the Americans say, kill two birds with one stone.

"Are you ready to take on our product?" Ivar said, when the snotty-wanna-be-drug-dealer answered.

"We can take whatever you can deliver. We have a pipeline in place–"

Ivar cut him off before the cursed little idiot could say more. "Phones are insecure. Mouth shut. Look for me. I am coming."

He laughed as another plan began to take shape in his head.

Chapter 5

Present day

Jack turned the corner and met Stan and Luke at the ocean's edge. He tried to dispel his anger. After all, he had finally found his match. It was only a matter of time before she was his.

As soon as the solstice was over, he'd make nice. Take her to the movies. Dinner. Together they'd work on her training. Maybe by next year she'd be ready. Better that, than the bleak future he'd envisioned before tonight.

Damn that he'd said the oath, though. Waiting for solstice to end was going to be hell on wheels. What was he thinking? He wasn't acting much better than Luke in that regard. Like the itch of poison ivy, the urge to mate was driving him mad. God help him. He might need to be handcuffed before week's end.

Although numbed by Olivia's tea, the nasty headache lingered. Jack got in Stan's car and they took Luke home.

Luke's parents doled out a litany of punishments at a decibel level that was probably illegal in the quiet beach community.

Jack winced when a couple of the points they spouted hit home. Something about never giving the oath to an unknown witch. Taking your time. Acting like an adult. *Crap.*

"They're laying it on pretty thick," Stan said, when they were back in the car.

"Better than getting arrested. She was only fifteen." Jack's voice came out more irritated than he meant.

"Luke didn't know that. You saw her. She looked a lot older. They should've carded her at the bar."

"What was Luke doing there in the first place? Drinking age is twenty-one in this state." Better to grouch at his cousin than continue to think about the healer with the big brown eyes. She was probably asleep by now, maybe even naked, with that mass of hair all tangled around her head.

"And we never did anything like that when we were his age?" Stan said with a smirk.

"That's different." The corner of Jack's mouth twitched but he managed not to smile.

"Right. We were perfect." Stan rolled his eyes and pulled out of the parking lot. "So, what happened back there? You didn't try anything with Olivia?"

"God, no. She's like my sister, and a healer to boot." He shrugged and looked out the window. "There's nothing worth recounting. Find a bar that's still open. I'm buying and I intend to tie one on until I can't feel anything."

Stan chuckled in approval and sped off towards their destination.

Jack adjusted himself and squirmed uncomfortably. He was still fucking hard. The woman's essence lingered on his clothes, her scent more intoxicating than Absinthe. Shit, he was so screwed. He called his brother, Josh, and told him to meet them at the small Irish pub.

The drinks numbed the migraine, but at the same time, it intensified his lascivious thoughts. He couldn't get the raven-haired witch out of his head. Who was she? How the hell was he going to convince her that she was the one? Especially if she wasn't trained.

The look of fear on her face when he'd slammed his fist into the wall stayed with him. *Shit. I'm such an ass.* He'd be lucky if she ever spoke to him again.

Stan and Josh watched him closely from across the table.

"What's going on with you?" Josh asked. "You never drink like this, especially not during solstice."

Jack shrugged, lifted his half-empty glass, and motioned to the bartender for another round.

"I think you've had enough." Josh pulled the glass out of his hand and shook his head at the bartender. "Let's get you home. My place is only a couple blocks from here. We can walk."

Stan leaned on Josh as they staggered out of the bar and onto the street. He groaned, "I'm going to feel like shit in the morning."

Josh laughed. "Serves you right."

"Shit." Stan stopped abruptly, grabbed Jack by the shirt, and stared down the street. Clouds of fog cleared for a moment and dark shadows appeared. "That's my brother, Kyle, isn't it?"

Jack tried to focus his drunken brain on the gang of swaggering young men.

"Look. It's our fucking leader, all fucked up." Kyle laughed, and his tattooed gang followed suit as if it was the funniest joke they'd ever heard. "Someone get you in the gut tonight?

I heard you had to find a healer for a baby-boy hit. Time you retired, old man."

Jack's chest tightened and his insides went cold. *That poisonous blast had come from Kyle?* He shook his head. *No way.* It wasn't in the nature of the cowardly drug addict to fight for leadership. What had changed in the equation? *Holy Goddess.* He should never drink like this. Couldn't connect the dots. Jack started to raise his hand to blast the little twerp into oblivion but Josh caught his hand.

"What do you want?" Josh moved forward.

"I wanted Jack to meet my, mate." Kyle grabbed a girl's ass with one hand, her tits with the other, and kissed her roughly. He hung his arm over her shoulder and smirked. "She augments me. *Perfectly.*"

Bloody hell. The little shit was serious. Jack glanced at the girl. She didn't look old enough to drive, let alone be someone's mate.

Jack didn't recognize her. She wasn't Iesco, so where the hell had she come from?

"Things are going to change around here." Kyle pointed at Jack and laughed. "I'm going to kill you. You're lucky you're too drunk and your family is with you, or I'd take the clan from you right now. C'mon, let's get out of here. The stench of old people is depressing."

Josh removed his hand from Jack's shoulder when the gang turned back the way they came.

"And here I thought I'd already had the worst fuckin' day of my life." Jack sighed, his brain amazingly sober.

Stan seemed a lot more sober, too. "You think he meant it, I mean about the girl being a match? If so, he could have a real go at you."

"I have no idea. It's possible. I didn't recognize that blast that hit me. I would've recognized Kyle's energy unless it's changed. We've fought often enough. If Kyle found a perfect match..." He scrubbed his hands over his face. "We're screwed."

"He's what? Nineteen?" Josh shook his head. "Finding a perfect mate already? Highly unlikely. Besides, he's so drugged up all the time, how would he even know?"

Stan smacked Jack on the back. "Whatever happens, you've got my support."

Jack didn't voice his doubts. "You know how it goes. If he calls me out for leadership, it's just us, one-on-one."

"You always win." Josh kicked a stone on the pavement.

"I've never had a serious challenger. If that was his new power that zapped me"—he shook his head—"I'm a dead man. You might want to think about getting your families out of town. Our clan may be shifting back to darker ways."

"I could shoot him for you." Josh tilted his head as if he was considering the option.

Jack almost laughed. That was one way to deal with the little bastard. If it didn't go against clan rules, he might take his brother up on his offer.

"Isn't there anyone else, even remotely related in the clan who could beat him in a duel?"

"Shit, Josh. I just don't know. You and Jase are the next most powerful. Either one of you ready to take him on?" Jack wished he could take the words back, but really? A man could endure only so much pressure, especially while inebriated.

Both Stan and Josh grimaced and walked the rest of the distance in silence.

When they reached the door to Josh's house, Jack said in a more conciliatory tone, "Let's sleep on it guys. Maybe we can think of something in the morning."

Jack already knew what he had to do. He fumbled for his cell phone and called the familiar number.

* * *

Zoe had just fallen asleep when Olivia's phone rang. She glanced at the clock and cursed into her pillow. It was three in the morning and she'd only been asleep for a couple of hours.

Through the thin walls, she heard Olivia's side of the conversation.

"Shit, twice in one night, Jack? Where are you? I'll be right down." Olivia let out an exasperated breath. "Then why the hell are you calling me at this fucking hour if you're not almost dead?"

Silence.

"...Shit, was she really that right for you?"

Zoe wished she could hear the answer to that question.

"...She's my friend, Jack, and some kind of remote cousin. She already has some serious emotional issues from childhood. I really don't want her to get hurt."

Wow. That was way too personal. Emotional issues? Zoe was going to give Olivia a piece of her mind in the morning. Her cousin made her sound like some kind of basket case. For all the crap she'd gone through as a kid, Zoe figured she was pretty fucking normal. At least she wasn't making shit up about witches and solstice.

Maybe it was time to pack up and go back to New York. *Screw these guys.*

She missed some of what was said next because Olivia had taken her voice down yet another notch.

"...And I will collect. I mean it. Don't mess with her. Ah huh. I know. G'night."

As soon as Olivia settled down, Zoe reached for her phone and whispered, "Call Nan."

The phone rang with that odd international ring, and then she heard Nan's voice. "Hey. What're you doing up so late?"

"You got a minute?"

"Sure, just a sec. Getting ready for work. London office expects me there by nine, but it's just a short walk. So what's up?"

"Are you sitting?"

"No...but I can put the seat of the john down."

"Do it."

A clatter was followed by a chuckle. "Okay, I'm sitting."

"I think I'm a witch." Even as it came out of Zoe's mouth, the words sounded downright insane.

There was a silence, which might just have been the connection, then a little giggle. "Not always. Just when you're PMS-ing and even then–"

"Not bitch. I said witch." Zoe tried to keep her voice to a hiss.

"Which one? Glinda or the wicked one?" Nan laughed so hysterically the phone distorted.

"Stop. This isn't funny. I'm not joking."

Her tone changed and the laughing stopped. "You're serious? What kind of shit were you into tonight? We've talked about the hard stuff–"

"Nothing. I promise. There's some weird shit going on here. And tonight something happened..."

Nan's voice grew tighter. "What's going on with you?"

Dark Vortex

Zoe tried to explain, but on the re-telling, it sounded even more surreal than when it happened. How does one explain the impossible?

"Listen. I know you're staying with your cousin who really believes she is a witch, and don't get mad, but you're in a vulnerable place right now."

"I'm not vulnerable. I hate it when you say that." Zoe sat up and stared out the window. The fog had lifted, the half-moon was bright, and the beach sand glistened like snow.

"Okay, let me put it this way. You're dealing with being abused as a kid. Something you've kept secret for years. Psychology books say it's a bad place to be. You'll give me that much?"

"Yeah. Sure. I guess." Zoe lay on her back, threw the pillow over her face, and wished she could suffocate herself.

"So, cults go after people like you. They smell it."

She removed the pillow so she could talk. "This is so not a cult."

"Did Olivia take you to a religious ceremony?"

Zoe moaned, turned onto her stomach, and sunk her face back into the pillow. She turned and said, "A celebration of the start of Solstice."

"Uh huh…and?

"Oh for crying out loud. I did not get indoctrinated." She almost forgot to keep her voice down.

Nan didn't. "What am I supposed to think? That you really can conjure up a vortex of purple energy or rather that you had a serious dose of hallucinogens? Don't eat anything else they offer you. Better yet. Go home."

"I can't. Remember stalker guy? Listen. I appreciate the advice. I'll be careful. And Nan?

"What?"

"Thanks."

"What are best friends for? Just one more thing."

"Sure."

"What's this guy's name?"

"Jack."

"Last?"

"Fia-something. I can't remember."

"Get it for me. I mean it."

Zoe promised she would and hung up the phone. She stared up at the ceiling and sighed. What was she supposed to do? Nan was right, any sane person would hightail it out of there first thing in the morning.

Her thoughts drifted to Jack. There was no denying there was something between them. He'd touched her, and for the first time she could remember, she hadn't drawn back at the physical contact. In fact, she'd actually liked it–craved it. The ache in her chest that never seemed to disappear, had for the briefest moment, dissipated.

Maybe she should give the man a chance.

No. She wasn't that insane.

Chapter 6

Jack wandered onto the height of the beach dune and sat down on a town bench. He sipped his coffee and let the morning breeze clear his hangover while the ocean churned. The sun burned through the haze, in promise of a beautiful day.

The lone figure by the ocean's edge cast long blue shadows on the sand. Tiny running shorts and an exercise bra left little to the imagination. She stretched her perfectly toned figure into impossible poses that he surmised must be yoga.

Which of those positions would she take to his bed?

Palms to her chest, she bowed to the sun, and then turned to run barefoot down the beach. A dark ponytail bounced behind her until it faded into the mist.

He picked up his cell phone and dialed his personal assistant. He braced for the assault and she didn't disappoint.

"My God, Jack. It isn't even seven yet. I thought you were taking a few days off. I was counting on a few hours of peace and–"

"Good morning to you, too." He smiled when he heard her huff on the other end. "I just have a couple things for you to take care of. First, did our guys find out anything on Zoe Burton?"

"Security put everything up on your FTP site. You can download at will."

"Thank you. Next. Are you listening carefully? Enact *Plan Juno*."

There was dead silence on the line, then a deep intake of breath. "Come again?"

"Everything you need is in that file. Most of the money transfers are set up to be automatic. Call our lawyers."

"But, Jack. We've got promises outstanding. Doctors without Borders, Big Brothers, Red Cross." Her voice rose a couple of octaves as she spoke. "We can't just pull the plug on all those people."

"Everything Janice. Make it safe. Now."

"What kind of danger are you in?"

"There's a challenger." Acid burned in his empty stomach, enhanced by worry and last night's booze. "I need to make sure that he doesn't get wind of the true value of our clan's assets."

"Is it that bad?"

"Just being prudent. We both knew that this might happen someday. I'll call you as soon as I have more. Keep everything business as usual."

Jack hung up and downloaded the file on Zoe. There was damn little there except for her hacking career. Not good. He needed more for what he had in mind.

He waited at the top of the dune until he saw Zoe's lithe figure jogging back down the beach. He watched as she dove into the frigid ocean. She ducked under a large wave, hopped up with another, and let out a shout when one almost knocked her over. Her joyful squeals made him chuckle.

It wasn't long before she toweled down, donned a tiny yellow sundress, and climbed the warming sand dunes towards him. A wet tangle of black hair cascaded in ringlets over her face, momentarily hiding her exotic features and thick soft pouty lips.

Her carefree walk changed to a cautious prowl when she spotted him. She came close, bent at the waist, and shook her head wildly.

"What're you doing here? How did you find me?" She paused and screwed up her face. "Damn it. Olivia told you where I was, didn't she? I'm going to kill her."

The breeze picked up and whipped her hair around her face and the sun ducked under a dark cloud. He wondered if she even knew how she affected the weather.

"I want you," he growled, trying to keep his demeanor casual, but even he could hear the dark hunger in his voice.

She dismissed him with a wave of her hand and bent at the waist to wrap a towel like a turban around her hair. The sun's rays came out again and sparkled on her still damp skin.

"We stopped. I want to try again." He took a step towards her.

"Where was that footnote, page two hundred and ninety-eight?" Her frown started to crack at the edges.

"You've been studying our clan?" It was all he could do to hide a satisfied smirk. He raised his eyebrows and stepped a little closer. Sand, salt water and a sexy scent assaulted his nostrils.

"I stayed up until two in the morning with the biggest book on sex since *Masters and Johnson*. You guys have an awful lot of mating rules. How do you keep track? It would seem to me like a little sex should be a lot easier than a three hundred page book."

Put like that, she made his chances sound slim.

"Those are just the rules for a few days out of the year. The rest of the time we're pretty much like everyone else."

"I highly doubt that," she scoffed. "Tell you what. I've got a suggestion. Why not subtract a few pages from that bible this year? Excuse me. I need to give one interfering-healer-witch a piece of my mind."

She turned on her heel and headed smartly towards the street.

Jack put his hands at her waist to hold her back. They gasped simultaneously and stared mutely, as fire and wind ran through them. Good God, when they finally got together, they were going to spontaneously ignite.

He waited for his racing heart to slow, but he couldn't let go. *Patience. Stakes are far too high to fuck up now.*

"Don't touch me," she whimpered, fear blazing in her eyes.

Shit. He let go and held his hands up in surrender.

He needed to fix this. Fast.

"Okay." He lowered his hand and extended it. "Let's take it from the top, like last night never happened. Hi, I'm Jack Fialko."

* * *

Zoe stared down at his outstretched hand and weighed the possibilities. His sleeves were rolled up, exposing the sinewy muscles of his forearms. Every time they touched, she melted like ice cream on a heated summer sidewalk.

Her knees knocked and her heart pounded. Better to just turn and walk away. Didn't she already have a full plate of emotional issues? But for the first time in her life, desire raced through her veins like a brush fire.

She took his hand. Sparks radiated through her arm, causing her body to tingle and her thighs to tense. She grew wet between her legs. The breeze blew off the ocean and further hardened the points under her wet bathing suit top. When she tried to pull out of his grip, he gently held her back.

"Let it happen, angel. Feel it." He whispered to her in the wind. "It's nature's way, witch to witch."

Heat raced down her back through her limbs. She stared up at him, feeling a mixed sense of vulnerability and power. Her body screamed for more. Why not just jump into bed with him? They were both grown adults. She might never feel this sexual pull again.

She shook her head and slipped her hand from his firm grip, common sense and self-preservation winning over lust.

"I'm Zoe Burton. Nice to meet you, Jack. But we're done here. I don't think I'm up for your weird courting. The way I recall, it seems to me you were pretty disinterested last night."

His stunned silence was the perfect opportunity to turn tail and run like hell. The small voice that had moments ago declared she needed to have sex was wrong. Very wrong.

Jack was on her heals in less than a millisecond. Before she knew what was happening his hands were around her waist. He held her with one hand strained against her lower back, while the other grasped the hair at the nape of her neck, his mouth so close to hers that she could feel his hot breath on her lips.

"Don't run from me, Zoe."

She started to protest, but his kiss silenced her words. He was surprisingly gentle. If the man had made any other move, she would have continued to resist, but the sweetness knocked her off balance.

Jack groaned, took her chin in his hand, and forced her to look into his eyes. "Are we settled on the question of whether or not I'm interested?"

His cock pressed against her stomach and his heart thumped in counterpoint to the wind and waves. She stared back into dark pools of desire. When his lips met hers again, she couldn't help but open up to him. His tongue swept into her mouth, creating a fire she couldn't control.

His gaze sharpened when they came up for air. "You can feel it. The connection. I know you can."

"Yes...No..." How was she to know anything when he was touching her? "I don't know."

He went for a deeper kiss, tasting and playing. His tongue did delicious things inside her mouth, and his teeth nipped at her lower lip. She arched against him, his touch overriding her common sense.

She couldn't think straight, and she sure as hell couldn't fight the attraction when he was kissing her. With every ounce of self-respect she had left, she pushed away, stumbling back on the warm sand.

He lowered his chin, eyes narrowing. "Zoe–"

"No." She held her hand up to stop his approach. "No more touching. No more kissing. Not until you tell me what's happening between us."

He sat on the bench's top edge, then patted the seat next to him. "Sit."

She carefully considered the request and took a seat as far away as possible.

He chuckled. "I don't bite."

Zoe frowned and shook the sand off her dress. "That remains to be seen."

The man kept smiling, and the dimple dug deeper into the muscle of his cheek. The wind tossed a roguish lock of hair over one eye.

"I assume Olivia gave you the book to read?"

She nodded and eyed him warily. "You really believe there is something between us?"

"You tell me." His voice went gravelly and low, like her favorite jazz sax player. "What causes that kind of want in the warring clan during the solstice?"

Zoe used her almost perfect recall. "Sexual attraction is at its fullest during the solstice when two from the same clan are well matched. In the rare case, two can be so well matched that their powers are permanently shared after coupling..." A light went on in her brain. "You think that you and I match? Are you nuts? Olivia told me you are chief or high lord or some such thing of the whole east coast."

"I usually settle for clan leader." He gave her a crooked grin. "As for the match, I feel it. You feel it. It is what it is."

Nan's voice from last night kept niggling at her conscience. "Uh-huh..."

"I did some studying of my own last night. That little black vortex you conjured, it's not even supposed to exist." He tilted his head and studied her. "Tell me, what's your lineage?"

Zoe gazed out onto the greenish-blue ocean. A seagull screamed in the distance over the crashing of the waves.

"Honestly? I have no idea and I'm still not convinced you guys didn't put something in my coffee last night."

He chuckled. "C'mon now. Get real. Tell me. What do you know about your parents?"

"Nothing. I'm adopted. After my parents died last year, I found my birth certificate along with this old letter. I connected with Olivia. We figure she's my second cousin." She watched some kind of grasshopper jump off the dune grass and onto the bench. "I hadn't heard of any of this until I came here."

He reached for her hand and she pulled away before he touched her. She needed a clear head if she was going to understand any of this.

"What about your powers? Didn't you suspect anything?"

"I've never had any...powers. I've never done anything like that tornado thingy before."

He frowned. "That doesn't make sense."

"Nothing about any of this makes sense," she snapped. She bit the inside of her cheek and sighed. "The book said you can only be from the Healer clan or the Warrior clan, but you can't be both."

The insect nodded his head in agreement. It took flight, landing by Jack's sandal foot, which was so damn masculine. He moved closer and their little toes touched. She almost moaned. It wasn't fair how much he affected her.

"You're right," Jack said, watching her with his sexy, lazy smile. "It's impossible. Except I know what I feel. You have to be warring or I wouldn't want you." He looked off into the distance, then turned back to her, his brows drawn down. "What did the letter say? The one you found with your records."

She shrugged. "It's in Romanian, to my birth mother from her aunt. It was dated from when I was a baby. Said something about hiding me. Wind talent. I honestly thought my translation was off. Either that or my great-aunt was off her rocker. That's all I've been able to find. Olivia agreed to help me look for more relatives online, but nothing so far."

The grasshopper jumped again with wings outspread, and landed behind them in the dunes. The blue sky promised a perfect summer day. She guessed they both enjoyed the harmony of the crashing waves against the shore because the ensuing silence was comfortable.

"I think I may have created a dust devil thingy once before when I was very young. I wasn't even sure, until yesterday, if my memories were real or a dream. It was like I was possessed or something."

"What do you mean?" His unblinking stare was unnerving.

"I'm not sure. I heard a voice in my head and remembered things from before I was adopted. I was maybe three or four. Yesterday was the first time I've ever recalled anything of my birth parents." She pulled her legs to her body when the breeze kicked up from the ocean and shivered.

"You're wet and cold. We should head back." He stood and held out his hand. "We can talk more, later."

"Talk?" she raised an eyebrow and stared at his outstretched palm.

"Yes, just talk." His voice was strained and tense. He dropped his hand. "Until you understand more about who you are, I promise–" He swallowed hard and grimaced. "No sex."

"Why?" The question sounded far too much like a whine on her own lips.

"The solstice madness will affect me and you'll have to fight me off to have sex. If you aren't strong enough, I could hurt you, badly. You could do the same to me. You need enough training for us to be safe."

Zoe shook her head, stood, and gave him a playful smile. "We could just wait five days and have normal, after-solstice sex."

"I've already said the oath." He moved towards her, slowly, like a predator intent on its prey. "We're going to finish this during solstice. Neither one of us will be content with anything less."

The dominance in his voice vibrated across her senses and she froze.

"Say you'll train with me." He trailed his knuckles down her cheek. The gold flecks in his light brown eyes seemed to flash with the heat that sparked between them. "Promise me."

"I promise," she whispered, but it came out more like a moan.

"Good." He stepped back abruptly. "Pack up. I'm taking you home with me."

"I didn't agree to come home with you."

He smiled wickedly. "Yes you did."

She tried to disagree but couldn't. "What did you just do? Was that some kind of spell? Damn you."

Jack smirked, looking pleased with himself. "I'll tell you later. Just know that I wouldn't have been able to convince you unless you really wanted it. Get moving. We have a lot to do today."

"I've got stuff to do. I can't just drop everything and stay with you. What about Olivia?"

"Liv will understand, and you can work at my house. I've got Wi-Fi."

She narrowed her eyes. How did he know she worked with computers?

"I'll make sure you have time to work." He shoved his hands in his pockets and shrugged. "You promised. You're coming. End of story."

Zoe was about to tell him to go fuck himself, but stopped dead cold when her gaze drifted to the beach. It couldn't be? Down by the ocean, picking up shells in a t-shirt and khaki shorts was the finger-gun-stalker-man from New York. Her stomach cramped. How the hell did he find her?

"What's wrong?" Jack gripped her hand and followed her gaze, but the man had disappeared behind one of the dunes.

She stood like an idiot for what felt like an eternity before she made up her mind.

"All right." Her voice trembled. "I'll go with you."

Chapter 7

Jack cringed. Maybe he'd been a little heavy-handed with Zoe, but his clan was depending on him. There was too much at stake.

The minute he'd parked in front of his family's beach house, her face had softened. Together they traversed the crushed stones, took the steps up the porch, and slid around the wicker furniture. She touched everything delicately, sighed happily, and his chest tightened.

"I spent my summers on this deck. Played games of monopoly with my siblings that lasted for days."

She smiled as if she got it. Jack opened the screen side door and led her up the narrow staircase. They went down a long hallway and he opened the door to the bedroom nearest his.

"My mom decorated this room. The whole house really."

She fingered the lacy materials like they were pirate booty.

Jack was about to say something about putting her clothes away, but noticed the battered knapsack. The small bag couldn't hold much.

"My sister says of all the rooms, this is the best. You can throw your stuff in here." He opened the closet door.

She gave him a small smile and his balls tightened. How in the world was he supposed to last five days?

"Want something to eat?" He fell back on his mother's favorite line. What was he now thirteen?

"Sure." She dropped her few meager belongings on the bed.

On the way down, she stopped, did a one-eighty on the landing, and gushed. "I've always wondered about the insides of homes like this. It's huge. Is this your place or are you renting? It's beautiful. I love it."

He laughed. Who knew? It wasn't his amazing charms, his portfolio, or stunning personality that won her over. It was the beach house.

"It's not mine, actually. Been in my family for generations. I have an apartment in Manhattan." They descended into the kitchen and she stood beside him as he poured coffee beans into a grinder. "Are you really hungry or will a snack do?"

"I'm starving."

He nodded in approval.

"What do you do for a living?" She leaned with her forearms on the island and watched him.

"I head up a few small startup security firms." He tried not to smile. There was some truth to that statement. He still couldn't believe she'd never heard of John James Fialko the third. Wasn't sure if that pleased him or pissed him off. "I assume you have another job, other than working part-time for Olivia?"

"Not at the moment. I was working for Amazon. I got bored with the whole thing. I'm between careers and trying to decide what I want to do next. Freelance consulting. You know how it is." She shrugged. "I have a few more web pages to write."

"I see." He raised an eyebrow at her, but she was already focused on her hands, ignoring his non-verbal inquest. No point in continuing that line of conversation right now. Once they mated, she'd have to stop with the whole illegal hacking career. "What can I get you to eat?"

She cocked her head to the side when he placed a frying pan on the stove. "You're going to cook? I thought we could go out..."

"I'm a pretty good cook, actually. Scrambled eggs okay?" Jack opened the door to the large modern refrigerator, pulled out a carton of eggs, and held them up to her.

She nodded.

Jack cracked two eggs using one hand and they dropped perfectly into the pan. Okay, he might have been showing off a little.

"I invited my sister, Kathy, over. I have no idea how to teach a grown woman how to come into her powers. She can help."

"Okay." She chewed on her bottom lip.

When he placed the eggs in front of her, she stared at him with her eyes all wide, and they started to water at the corners.

Jack looked down at the plate and frowned. "What? Too dry? I can try again."

She actually started to cry. Not the big sobbing thing. No. Just a couple of tears that she angrily wiped away with the back of her hand.

"Sorry. That was just really nice of you. I mean people make other people breakfast all the time. Right?"

"Yeah, they do. What's wrong, Zoe?" Jack sat down next to her, careful not to touch her.

"It's stupid, really."

"Not if you're crying."

She turned away. "I just don't remember anyone ever making me breakfast before."

"Never?"

With her back still to him, she made a little negative motion with her head. Against his better judgment, Jack moved closer, kissed her neck, and breathed in her scent. She still smelled like the ocean, fresh and salty. Like mother earth. Blood rushed south and he quickly put some space between them.

Fuck, what was going on with him? Mating was all about the sex. He shouldn't care whether she'd ever had breakfast served. *Damn.* His head suddenly felt screwed on all wrong.

He wracked his brains for words of comfort but his tongue stuck to the roof of his mouth.

"Let's just wait over here in the parlor for a few minutes. My sister should be along any minute." *Great job comforting her, Jack. What a blithering idiot.*

He got her situated and made a beeline up the stairs towards a cold shower. That was probably all he needed. Then he'd be fine. On the way up, he heard his niece babbling on the front porch. *Shit.* He rushed back down the stairs, just as his sister entered.

"Hello beautiful ladies." Jack gave each a kiss on the cheek.

"Is it true?" Kathy caught his eye and shifted the baby onto her other hip. "The little weasel Kyle threw a couple of cowardly shots at you last night. Did he really almost kill you? Then challenged you? What're you going to do?"

Jack held up his hand. "How did you hear all this?"

"The whole clan knows. It doesn't take a brain surgeon to put two and two together. Kyle is after your leadership." Her face grew pale as she spoke. "The last time you two fought, you barely came out on top. Has he really found a perfect mate?"

"Don't panic. I have a plan and you and Yolanda are part of it."

At the sound her name, the baby squealed, "Ya, ya, ya, ya." She reached her chubby arms to him and he happily took her over in the crook of his arm. She kicked her legs into his stomach and laughed at some big 'ol baby joke known only to her.

His sister peered into his face. "You really look like shit, you know."

"Thanks. You always know just the right thing to say. Follow me. I want the baby to play with this woman I met last night." He moved Yolanda onto his hip and she pulled at his hair, so he conjured an imaginary small ring of keys and let them float just beyond her grasp.

"A woman?" Kathy frowned.

"Trust me."

She followed him into the sunny parlor.

"Do you think this is a good idea? We've generally kept her away from the public until she gets some of her more interesting talents under control."

"Her magic won't be a problem. I'm counting on some sparks." Jack laughed and lifted the baby high into the air and she squealed.

Zoe must have splashed some water on her face because instead of a red nose and puffy eyes, she gave them all a bright smile. The sun came through the window making her eyelashes sparkle with beads of water. It took some effort to look away.

"Kathy, meet my untrained mate choice, Zoe Burton."

Dark Vortex

* * *

Zoe's mouth dropped open at Jack's introduction. *Untrained mate choice?*

Kathy gave her brother an incredulous stare and mouthed, 'Are you insane?' Then turned back to Zoe with syrupy sweetness. "So nice to meet you."

Zoe wasn't that clueless. She heard the insult in Kathy's tone but the baby was sugar-sweet. The cutie waved her pudgy little fists, and to Zoe's surprise, pushed a burst of energy–and a wet magic baby kiss–into the air. When it landed on her face, Zoe tentatively tried to blow the same energy back.

A slight breeze blew across the room and landed on the baby's forehead. The baby giggled, clapped her hands, and a torrential rainstorm covered the parlor, complete with thunder and lightning. It appeared to soak her audience.

"No." Kathy lightly tapped the baby's hands. "Make nice day. No rain." She cleared away the storm with a wave of her hand, turned to Zoe, and muttered a snotty, "Sorry."

Jack laughed it off and shook his head. He stared Zoe up and down until her panties all but melted off. "I'll leave you ladies alone."

She blushed as he ran up the stairs.

"Babies can really do magic?" She tried to break into the silence which his sister, obviously, had no intention of doing.

"It's an illusion. What are you, human?" Kathy's face showed every ounce of disdain possible.

She wasn't sure how this kind of training was going to be helpful. What was up with the hostility? After all, none of this was her idea.

"Jack called you his mate," Kathy said, placing Yolanda on the floor and scattering toys around her.

Zoe shrugged. "He seems to think so."

"*Untrained* mate?" Kathy's eyes were large now, as if she had just had a terrifying thought. "Did he say the oath?"

"Yes."

"Shit." Kathy looked like she was about to burst a gasket.

Zoe added quickly, "But it wasn't his fault. He just assumed I believed in your ways. I don't."

The baby stood on shaky legs, then sat down with a thump and giggled. Moving her pudgy arms in the air, she made giant spiders appear.

Zoe cringed and reminded herself that it was only an illusion. She was never going to get used to this.

Kathy cleared away the insects. "He's holding off the madness until you have some chance of mating? That's why he wants me to train you?"

Zoe shrugged and studied one of the many ferns in the solarium.

"Why on earth did you agree to this?"

The baby began to cry at the harsh sound of her mother's voice. Kathy picked her up and soothed her, all the while shooting eye darts.

"He was the one who tricked *me* into coming here. I didn't want to come. He followed me to the beach like...like some kind of stalker."

"Did he tell you *why* he thinks he needs you?"

Zoe felt her blood go cold. Of course, there was a reason. She shook her head.

"He needs you to augment his powers because his cousin is threatening to kill him." Kathy stood and paced back and forth over the hardwood floors with the baby bouncing at her waist. "Kyle's into some very bad shit. Last time they dueled, Kyle almost won. Now the little twerp is claiming he found a perfect match." Kathy stared daggers at Zoe. "Do you understand what this means? If Jack doesn't find the same, he won't survive. Last night's sneaky blast was just a sampling of what Kyle will do."

"So if I'm not his match, then he could die?" Cold shock crawled through her body.

Kathy nodded with a grim face. "My brother's desperate and not in his right mind."

Zoe frowned. She wondered about her own state of mind. How had she let him talk her into this? She should leave now, before things got any weirder. She didn't owe these people anything. She glanced at the door and thought about making a beeline for it.

"Jack thinks you're his match, but what do you think?" Kathy let out an exaggerated sigh.

Zoe blinked and licked her lips. Just the thought of the man made her toes curl and her skin tingle.

"You like him?" Kathy raised an eyebrow.

"There's definitely something between us. Ever since he first touched me at Olivia's shop–"

"*You* were there? My brother Josh said that some other healer saved Jack last night, not Olivia."

"Yeah, that was me."

"But you're warring, not healing." Kathy's brows drew together sharply. "You can't be both."

"That's what I keep hearing." Zoe shrugged. She seemed to be doing that a lot lately.

"How'd you heal him?"

"I–" Zoe cringed. It sounded surreal to say it aloud. "I created this black and purple-dust-devil-thingy."

"Whoa." Kathy stepped away with fascination and a bit of fear in her eyes. "Vortex energy. I've heard bedtime stories, but no one's ever seen it, let alone conjured it."

"I don't even know how I did it. Or even if I could do it again."

Kathy paced, bounced, and then paced some more. She refused to make eye contact. Finally, she stopped and looked at Zoe. "I can try to help. I don't know how much I can teach you in such a short time, but I can try."

Zoe blinked in surprise. If Kathy was willing to train her, then things must be bad. "If Kyle's as bad as you say he is, it's not good for Jack."

"No." Kathy's lips thinned. "It's not good for any of us."

Chapter 8

Three months prior
Zoe waited at Nan's apartment door, her heart still thumping like crazy. Her best friend appeared in a simple black suit and silk shirt. The long white sleeves and neck scarf covered most of the tats. All of the pink hair stripes were gone, along with nose, eyebrow, and lip rings.

"Did someone die? You look so…different." Zoe followed Nan into the small apartment, carrying a bag of their favorite Chinese takeout.

"Had a job interview today."

"No way! You swore you'd never go legit." Zoe gave Nan an awkward hug. More like a pat on the back, but it was a start.

Nan raised her eyebrows and removed round aluminum containers. Somehow, she found a spot for paper plates between the laptops, printer, and monitors. There was an external hard drive, and a couple other electronic devices that Zoe didn't recognize on the chairs as well.

"First things first." Nan placed a pile of textbooks on the floor and sat. "What're you working on that would send some stalker after you? I thought we agreed that we weren't going to take any more questionable jobs unless we talked it out."

"I swear I've done nothing since my parents died."

"Any freelance jobs on Craigslist?" Nan's intense stare would make her an awesome cop someday.

"Absolutely not. I'm working for that place, Broad Street Computer Security. They have real clients, real paperwork. I even filled out a W2 form. They love me there. Might even give me a raise. Besides, I need the insurance for–" Zoe swallowed hard and looked down at her hands. "My therapist. You know I wouldn't jeopardize that."

"So when did you first notice this guy following you?" Nan slipped the chopsticks out of their paper, and separated them with a click.

"I don't know…" Zoe found the least occupied chair, moved the stack of papers, and sat. "Maybe a couple weeks ago, but who knows how long he was following me before that."

"Okay, download."

"I noticed the guy when I left Broad Street. Second time this week that he's been waiting for me after work." The tremor in her hand made chopsticks an impossibility. She grabbed a fork from the drawer and plopped back down. "So I picked up my pace and thought I'd lost him. but all of a sudden he's like right behind me. His hand almost grabbed onto my arm. He would've too, if this big guy hadn't pushed him aside when I screamed."

Nan shook her head and frowned.

"But that's not the worst of it. I'm sitting on the subway and look out the window and there he is on the other side of the plate glass, just staring all weird-like. Creepy as hell. He makes a gun with his fingers. One thumb up and the index finger pointing." Zoe emulated the virtual gun and pointed it at Nan. "And then he mouths the word, 'Bang.' I was shaking like crazy but I had my cell phone in my hoodie. So I snapped his picture." She pulled her phone out and opened the photo. "I went three stops in the wrong direction before coming back here, just to make sure I wasn't followed."

Nan stretched to see the shot on Zoe's phone. "Too bad. He's pretty hot. Nice suit, too."

Zoe rolled her eyes. "He's not hot, he's a nutcase."

"Send me the picture. I just got access to some pretty cool facial recognition software. We can try it out."

Zoe raised her eyebrows and sent the photo to Nan's email. "Facial recognition software?"

"Relax. I've been helping out NYPD with some terrorist shit. They're the ones that called *me* in."

Nan wiggled her eyebrows and it finally dawned on Zoe what was up.

"Thus, the suit? Oh my God." Zoe squealed, jumping up and down in her seat. "You had an interview with NYPD?"

"Not exactly." Nan stood, then twirled in front of her. "Do I look FBI?"

Zoe snorted. "Except for the sword tattoo up the side of your neck."

"That one *is* hard to hide." Nan grinned, pulled off her scarf, and unbuttoned her shirt, revealing her favorite camouflage cutoff tank top. "The department I'm interviewing for doesn't seem to mind the body art."

"Why didn't you tell me?" Zoe stabbed at a chicken ball.

"Happened last week. I haven't had a chance." Nan waved her chopstick in the air. "There was a terrorism attempt that

I found out about. I was on site with a team, like in a big war room, helping out."

"Were you snooping through government files again?"

Nan wiggled her eyebrows.

Zoe laughed and swallowed the wrong way. She grabbed a glass of water, gulped, and sat back down. "What if they caught you?"

"Never gonna happen." Nan put down her chopsticks and typed at lightning speed on her keyboard. "Anyhow, looked like the city needed my help, so I pretended to be a terrorist."

Zoe froze mid-bite. "You pretended to be a fucking terrorist?"

Nan shrugged and popped a chicken ball in her mouth, chewed, then smiled. "I just bought way too much fertilizer and some other stuff that I knew would flag me. And it did. I got arrested."

"That's kinda over the top, even for you."

"I know, right?" Nan laughed. "There was a maniac hypnotizing people online. Friggin' incredible. I caught his site and recorded it when no else could. I can't even talk about it. But my awesome hacking skills helped them catch the bad guys, and I met this hot cop." Nan closed her eyes with a dreamy look that Zoe had never seen her use before. "The guy is unbelievable in bed."

"I leave you alone for a few days and this is what happens?" Zoe exhaled and it came out with a whoosh.

"Finding the bad guys is way more fun than *being* the bad guy." Nan began to close up the leftover food in the containers and put them in the refrigerator. She pulled out a bottle of wine from the bottom rack. "Hey, look what I found. Want a glass?"

Zoe nodded, found a couple glasses, and took them over to the counter. She poured, took a sip and grimaced at the cheap wine.

Nan sat down on the old grey couch and patted the spot beside her. The only other furniture that could fit in the tiny room was a coffee table and a wall with a monitor. Instead of sitting next to Nan, Zoe perched on the edge of the couch.

"So, while we wait to see if something pops up on your stalker, did you find your great-aunt yet?"

"You mean the witch?" Zoe rolled her eyes and laughed. "That was one strange weekend."

"I hardly remember much of it." Nan smirked. "Or your parent's funeral. We drank what was left of their wine collection?"

"I'm surprised we finished before the cops locked us out of the house. How the hell does anyone rack up over a million in debt?"

"Probably 'bout a hundred thou' a year for ten years...." Nan chuckled.

"Ha. Ha. Thanks for the math lesson. But I *am* glad we got my papers out of the filing cabinet. Otherwise, I wouldn't have even known where to start looking for my biological family."

"I still can't believe they never told you, you were adopted. Your parents had some serious issues..." Nan stopped as if she'd stepped in a pile of dog shit. "Oh Zoe, I'm so sorry."

Crap. Here it comes. Zoe tried to swallow back the horrible memories, the anxiety that formed a baseball size lump in her throat. But just as her therapist, Doctor Larry, had explained, the more you try to stop it, the more it'll attack. She let a few pictures of her past dribble into her mind like a leaky faucet.

Man. Her father was so screwed up. What kind of pervert got jacked up over touching a kid?

When the memories faded, Nan was there, watching her patiently.

"Do you want to talk about it?"

Zoe shook her head, then took a deep sip of her wine.

"Okay." Nan gave her a sad smile.

"Don't do that pity thing. I hate that almost as much as the memories. Dammit. How long you think it's going to take before I don't feel so shitty every time someone mentions his name? It's like having my own personal Susquehanna Hat Company."

"I don't know." Nan put her hand on Zoe's leg, then drew it back when Zoe flinched.

"I didn't find anything else about the..." Zoe made air quotes. "Witch. But, I did connect with a distant cousin on Facebook. She wants me to come visit."

"Hmmm...Maybe that's our answer to the stalker. You can work remotely, right?"

"I guess." Zoe frowned and glanced down at her wine. "I can ask."

"I think you should clear out of town for a little bit."

"I'd miss you." She hated how whiney she sounded, but the thought of not having Nan to talk to left an empty space in her chest. "You're my only family now."

"And you're my little sister, but I'd feel better knowing you were out of the city because I think my new job might be sending me overseas."

Zoe's mouth dropped open in shock. "So soon? For what?"

"Well they didn't tell me exactly, so I kind of snooped around."

"Shit, Nan, you hacked into the FBI? Your would-be employer?"

"Well, let's just say that some of the guys just happened to be logging in as I walked by, and I just happened to remember their keystrokes. I found an empty computer on the way to the lady's room."

Zoe held out her empty glass for Nan to fill, and shook her head. "So where are they sending you?"

"Looks like Afghanistan. There seems to be an influx of slave trade to the U.S. that we're supposed to track." Nan held up her hand when Zoe started to protest. "I'll be fine. Trust me. Now let's pick a movie to watch while we wait for the computer to identify your stalker guy."

Zoe gave her friend a rare hug and sat down on the couch. Three movies and two bottles of wine later, they fell asleep.

A little after midnight, the computer program gave up with an alert, PERSON NOT FOUND.

Chapter 9

Present day

Ivar looked out his bedroom window that towered above the beach below. The place had cost him ten-thousand a week. Just to watch water and sand? Bah.

He picked up his cell phone and spoke in his native tongue to his leader, "I've found the witch in a small burg by the ocean."

"Good. When can I expect you back? I'll have a car waiting for you at the airport."

"Calm yourself, Gregor. There are complications."

"Isn't there always?" Gregor sounded more irritated than usual. "I expected this done by now. If you had just grabbed her in New York, you'd be home and I'd be enjoying the fruits of your labor. I've been more than patient. There is much at stake, cousin. If you cannot handle it, I will."

"I'll handle it in *my* time." He slowly padded over to the coffee maker. He wasn't about to admit that the woman had proved more resourceful than he'd predicted. Even without the use of her powers. Imagine what she could do when the curse was lifted.

"It's *my* decision, and by being overly cautious, you missed your best opportunity to bring her home to me! That's the trouble with you, Ivar, you're too cautious."

"And you are too reckless, cousin. I'm here. You're not. Stay out of it. She's my niece and I will choose how to get her home." Ivar spat and made an ancient curse. He filled the glass jug, put in the stupid pouch, and pushed the on button. The coffee would taste like shit. Leave it to the Americans to ruin even the most basic of foods. "I am merely giving you the courtesy of updating you."

"You promised her to me." The man's voice was an irritated whine.

"You're impatience will only get you into trouble." Ivar made a guttural sound at the back of his throat. "As long as I am here, there are some things I'd like to get set up. There is potential for money to be made. A clan I might like to have as my own."

Ivar picked up his binoculars and scanned the area. The beach was empty, except for a few people with fishing poles. Several others sat in wooden benches at the top of the dunes.

"What if she mates in the meantime?"

"Makes no difference in the long run, does it? If she mates well, it could be better for all of us to wait for the child of that union. Better to get more pure blood, no? We're not even sure how the Romanians managed a half-breed. Another generation removed would do well to remove the taint. You need to think more in terms of the future of the clan, not just the worm between your legs."

"Are you reneging on your promise?" Gregor sounded alarmed.

"Relax. When have I ever let you down? You can have her when I get home. You already have too many whores and your wife to please. You can't keep the half of them happy."

"Bastard. You know what I want. I want to mate with the witch. I want that fucking vortex in my own line."

Ivar snorted and put on his sneakers. "You have grandsons almost old enough to bed the woman. Give her to one of them. Better for us to find a powerful mate for her here and take the child."

"Bah. None of them are powerful enough. Weaklings, all. They would never match her. We will lose the vortex for all of our descendants. You may be the last one left. Think on that."

Ivar walked out of his colossal rented house, down the steps over the dunes.

"Does she have a clue of her origin?' Gregor had a mouth that would not end.

"No. The couple we put in charge of her was careful to keep her caged and ignorant."

"Too careful. We almost lost her. What were they thinking?"

"Who knows, perhaps the man you put in charge was waiting to mate with her, himself. Give me time and I will bring her home." Ivar sneered into the phone. "And what of your part in this? Did you find the sister of the girl's grandmother? The abhorrent healer that caused this disaster to begin with? Without her, we won't know if our seed will take."

"Not yet. But I will."

"Ha. I'll bet you five thousand rubles that I will be home and fucking your daughters before you find her."

"Bastard. Sniff around any of them again and I'll cut your balls off."

Ivar laughed. "As long as I'm here there is potential retail business. Check my secure FTP site for details. You're going to need more mules. This clan has some enterprising poppy potential. Philadelphia is very close and New York City not many kilometers away from that."

With that, he hung up the phone. Gregor would go to his FTP site and see the money to be made, and happily offer up perhaps more than one daughter as a reward. Meanwhile, Ivar would need to finish what he started last night without inciting a clan war—at least not yet.

Chapter 10

Zoe rummaged through her small knapsack of clothes and let out a frustrated breath. Her anxiety was through the roof. Jack had invited his entire family over for a backyard barbeque, and after pressing him for how many people that included, she was appalled to find out that it wasn't just his immediate family, but aunts, uncles, and even distant cousins.

She could hear the caterers setting up below her window. Closing her eyes tightly, she sat down on the edge of the bed and tried to come up with an escape plan.

Why had she agreed to this?

She tossed the old knapsack on the floor and fell back on the bed, burying her face in a pillow. It was bad when even *she* knew that worn-out jeans and an oversized t-shirt were inappropriate.

Desperate, she called Olivia.

"Is Jack treating you okay?" In the background, the cash register clanged and a small child let out a wail of protest.

"Actually, I haven't seen much of him. I've been with Kathy and the baby and now I'm invited to a barbecue."

"And?"

"Can I borrow something to wear?" Zoe laughed nervously and paced across the floor of the small bedroom.

"Of course. What're you doing with your hair and makeup?"

Zoe breathed a deep sigh. "Honestly, I haven't even thought about it."

"Say no more. I'm coming right over."

Zoe stood, tilted the old-fashioned mirror on the center hinge, and did an honest assessment of her style, or rather lack of it. She didn't even own a hair dryer, let alone a pile of makeup. She still had on the jeans and oversized t-shirt she'd donned in haste this morning. Her long dark hair had escaped from the bun she'd held in place with a rubber band and pencil.

She stuck her tongue out. *Seriously? Whatever.* Looking too good only attracted trouble, like stalkers, or rapists or…molesters. Damn it. The reality of why she hid behind baggy shirts and thick-rimmed glasses hit her like a slap across the face. Yet another unnatural behavior based on her fucked-up childhood. Time to let that one go.

Zoe looked out the window just in time to see Jack, bare-chested and gleaming with sweat, saunter past the cottage steps towards the beach for an after-run swim. Lust flared, and for a second, Zoe swore he stole her breath. She wanted him so badly it made her stomach twist in knots.

It wasn't like she hadn't had boyfriends before. There had been plenty of guys who had been interested, but when it came to sex, she'd always felt like a cold fish. She'd thought something was permanently broken inside of her, had even started to accept it, but now…

Now there was Jack.

* * *

A couple hours later, Zoe hardly recognized the woman in the mirror. Her dark hair was pulled into an up-do with a few layers curling around her face. Enormously long lashes framed brown, smoky eyes, and instead of blotchy patches, her skin exuded radiance, health, and shine. Her lips were stained and plumped red, matching the nails on both feet and hands.

She was almost teary when she turned to Olivia.

"Don't cry, damn it, your mascara will run." Liv laughed, and gave Zoe a small hug.

"I'm nervous," Zoe said, studying her reflection. The low cut jeans and tight t-shirt left her feeling exposed.

"You should be." Olivia tapped her on the cheek, forcing Zoe's focus away from the mirror. "Jack wants to mate with you, and in his twisted warrior mind, that's even more binding than love and marriage."

"He's just doing this so he doesn't lose his position in his clan...he needs me."

"You think that's all there is?" Olivia frowned and placed her hands on her hips. "Then what?"

Zoe shrugged. "Then, whatever happens, happens."

"I don't think you're getting this. The warring clan believes that if you match, you mate for life. Forever. Get it? You're tied to him *forever*, which is a lot more than a little piece of legal paper. You'll never get rid of him. You won't even want sex with anyone else for the rest of your life." Olivia frowned and crossed her arms over her chest. "Are you okay with that?"

Forever. Instead of scaring her like Olivia intended, the thought warmed her insides. Would he really want to stay with her? She doubted it. She hadn't ever had a relationship last more than a few months. There was still the little girl inside of her that wanted forever, that craved the happily ever after.

"I told Jack I'd try," Zoe said, softly.

"Maybe you're both more suited than I thought." Olivia laughed, then grabbed her purse and makeup bag off the bed. "You're both equally hardheaded."

"Thanks," Zoe grunted.

"Relax." Olivia opened the bedroom door. "I've known Jack's family for years. They are intense, but once you get to know them, you'll really like them."

"But will they like me?" Zoe muttered, gathering her courage, and descending the steep stairs. Thankfully, the first floor was empty, except for the kitchen help. She scooted by them, paused at the screened door, and froze. The backyard was already way too crowded.

Jack spotted her and his expression darkened. He stalked towards her and pulled her into the shadows.

"Are you purposefully torturing me, Zoe? These jeans are way too low, and this t-shirt has nothing to it." Jack's hands circled her waist.

Goose bumps raced up and down her arms, and heat sizzled where his skin touched hers.

He chuckled and whispered into her ear, "Every time I see you, you morph into a completely different creature, each one more beautiful than the last."

"Would you rather have me dressed like last night, in sweats and fuzzy slippers?"

"No, I'd rather have you naked under me so I could sink into you all night." His voice took on an edge, his eyes went dark and his brows furrowed. He cursed and stepped away, his fists clenched.

"This was a bad idea. I'll go change..." Zoe swallowed hard.

"I'm sorry." Jack grabbed her hand. "Don't change a thing. I had no idea how tough this was going to be." His fingers rasped across the stubble on his chin and a dazzling yet fake smile emerged. "Let me start over. Would you like a drink?"

She nodded and let him lead her through the maze of people.

Over fifty guests gathered. Torches were lit to keep the mosquitoes at bay, and twinkling lights wrapped the perimeter of the yard. Young teens in black jeans and white shirts appeared out of nowhere, passing plates of hors d'oeuvres.

In the center of the lawn, an ice sculpture of a dolphin, sweated on a long table, surrounded by geometric patterns of cheeses, seafood, and cold salads. It would be a crime to take anything and unbalance the perfection.

Near the front of the house, one of the caterers operated a gas fired grill. Parents with young children in tow, lined up for hot dogs and burgers.

After enduring their stares, and giving polite little nods, Zoe decided it was easier to focus on Jack. He was dressed in typical careless beachwear, ocean-weathered ripped jeans and a loose white shirt. Some kind of rune tats showed on his tanned, exposed shoulders and his still damp hair curled under at the nape of his neck. She reached to touch a lock, but then thought better of it.

"I watched you for a while with my sister from an upstairs window. You're a natural." He poured himself a foamy brew from a metal cylinder, then picked up a corkscrew. "White?"

She nodded and all but drooled over his bulging biceps.

He slowly pulled the cork out of the bottle, glanced up, and smirked. He did this muscle-man show by squeezing his biceps a couple more times until Zoe laughed aloud. "You want some of that?"

"Actually, I do." She clamped her mouth shut, but it was too late, the words were already out. She looked down at the ground and chewed on the inside of her cheek.

He placed a finger under her chin and forced her to look up. "Don't mess with me Zoe, unless you're ready to go upstairs and finish what we started yesterday."

"Sorry." Why was she apologizing? For wanting the man, and being honest? She didn't know who she was more frustrated with, herself or Jack.

He shifted back to a forced congeniality and said loudly enough so others could hear, "You ready to meet some more of my family?"

She chewed on her lip and nodded.

Jack led her towards a group of people waiting for introductions. Her hands got all sweaty. Everyone was staring. Watching. Panic clawed at her throat. She wasn't good in large groups. They seemed to suffocate her.

The gate out of the yard was just a few feet away. She could run back into the house or back to Olivia's.

Jack followed her gaze and his grip tightened on her hand. "You're doing fine. Just relax."

A middle-aged woman stood up from her lawn chair when she saw them approach.

"Mom." Jack greeted her with a kiss on the cheek, then pulled back and placed his arms around Zoe's shoulder. "I'd like you to meet Zoe Burton."

Zoe smiled nervously, feeling more like the outsider than ever.

"So lovely to meet you. I'm Corinne." The woman leaned in and kissed Zoe's cheek, then pulled back to examine her. "My son tells me you're royalty? This was all so unexpected. Where have you been hiding?"

Zoe's mind went blank and Jack stepped in without missing a beat. "Ah, you know how New York is, mother." He raised his eyebrows as if that explained everything. "I've downloaded her lineage. You should have an email already. I hate to brag, but she's a treasure who's been hiding right in our midst."

"If you'll excuse me," Zoe said. "I'm suddenly not feeling well."

She turned on her heel and fled through the crowd.

Jack caught up with her, gripped her wrist, and spun her around. "What's wrong with you?"

"Why would you lie to her?"

"I'm not lying." He glanced up at the small throng of people that was beginning to gather around them. With a shake of his head, he led her down to the beach.

"I opened your adoption papers and then emailed everything to the clan's archive bureau. What I said was true."

"You know who my parents were?" Zoe wrapped her arms around her chest and shivered, numbness crawling up her fingers and arms.

"Some of it was guess work." He shoved his hands in his pockets. "Your father had to be Russian. That's the only clan with vortex talent. The oldest, most powerful line of witches in the world. They're also very secretive. There's no way that clan would've let you out of their sights. Somehow they lost you."

Zoe sat down in the cool sand and felt her throat construct.

"I'm sorry, angel. I forget that this must be pretty difficult for you." He sat down beside her.

"Did you find anything about my mother?" Zoe held her breath.

"Not sure yet. If the letter you have from your great aunt was accurate, we know your mother must've been at least part healer. That would make her the only known power-wielding half-breed in over a century, maybe longer. That's how you were able to heal me." He reached for her hand. "You okay?"

She nodded. *No not really.* How was she supposed to process everything she'd learned in the last two days? And now she was being asked to make a commitment to a man she barely knew.

His thumb turned her chin to meet his interrogating gaze. "Talk to me."

Zoe melted into the dark pools of his eyes. His mouth was so close. Could she really do forever with this man?

"Have you ever been in love?" she asked.

His frown lines grew deeper. "Yes."

That wasn't the answer she'd expected. She wasn't sure why it surprised her, but it did.

"Have you?" He tilted his head and waited patiently for her answer.

She looked at him and answered honestly. "No."

He studied her, but didn't respond.

"Does it worry you, that this mating will bind us for life?" she asked, digging her toes into the cool sand. "That we might never...love each other?"

Jack sighed and his face relaxed. "Mating is better, Zoe. People who fall in love can just as easily fall out. I'm offering you forever. I'll never leave you. You'll never leave me. It's as simple as that. Don't make this harder than it is."

Zoe glanced over her shoulder at the party. "I don't fit in here."

"Tell me, angel, are you having second thoughts?" Jack cupped her cheeks and a shadow of fear fell over his face.

"Maybe. Aren't you? Forever sounds like an awfully long time."

Jack cursed, pulled her onto his lap, and his lips claimed hers. She moaned and he reacted by holding her tighter. Electricity stirred the air, and a gentle breeze wrapped around them. Every neuron in her body seemed to fire at once.

"Would that be the worst thing?" His voice was husky and warm. "To feel like that for the rest of your life and know I'll always feel the same for you?"

When she was in his arms, it was hard not to agree with his logic, or lack thereof. All her life she'd let fear rule her thoughts, her actions. When she was in his arms, she could feel herself letting go. It was the closest thing to love that she'd ever felt. How could she not want more?

"I have to let you go now, Zoe."

"Not yet. Just a few more minutes." She pressed closer to him, needing more.

"A few more minutes and I'll take you right here." He smiled and his dimple showed.

"Okay, just do it. I mean it. Why not? Let's go upstairs." She had to have him. Now. Here on the beach, if that's what it took.

"Are you really ready?" He made a painful moan, and his eyes, blackened by wide pupils, looked straight through her.

She glanced down. "I don't know, but this is killing me. I've never wanted anyone or anything so bad."

"Honey, look at me." His fingers lifted to smooth back the hair that had fallen over her cheek. "I thought you were going to give it one more day of training?"

She closed her eyes so she wouldn't have to look into those deep pools of desire. If she jumped in, she knew she would never be able to find her way out. There was no way to ignore his erection that pressed into her hip. God it felt so hard, so good.

"I can't be strong for both of us much longer." He moved her onto the sand beside him, then stood up. He shoved his hands in his pockets and stared down at her, his breathing rapid. "Just tell me, are you ready to fight? If you are, just say the word. We'll go upstairs right now."

Zoe tried to find some semblance of sanity. Was she honestly ready to put Jack's life and the future of his family in her hands? She couldn't even conjure a tiny dust devil.

"No." The word caught in her throat. She stood and turned before he could see the tears welling in her eyes. She started back towards the house, both relieved and disappointed when Jack didn't follow after her.

Chapter 11

Zoe ran through the crowded yard and exhaled heavily when she made it to the front of the house without being stopped by any of Jack's relatives. Her chest felt like it was crushing her lungs. She needed space and time to think.

By the time she stopped running and glanced around, she was disoriented.

"Perfect," she muttered, still breathing heavy. She sat down on the curb and put her forehead to her knees. Could this day get any worse?

She looked up when a car took a sharp corner, squealing its tires. The black sedan stopped within inches of her knees and a dark figure shot out of the driver's side.

Shadows hid the man's face, but his intent was clear. Zoe screamed when he jumped towards her. He covered her mouth with rough fingers, and dragged her by the waist. She kicked and clawed, but the man only grunted.

Something hard hit the side of her face and her knees gave out.

The driver threw her into the back seat and raced to the front. Tires spun, gravel ticked the windows, and burned rubber stunk up the car. Outside, streetlights blurred by. Inside, another man bound her wrists with plastic ties that cut her flesh.

Rage and terror whipped through her system. This couldn't be happening. Her heart raced and she squirmed towards the door. The latch was under her fingertips when the childproof locks engaged with a sharp click. *Oh God. She was so screwed.* In the rearview mirror, black, emotionless eyes stared back.

A tattooed man wearing a sick grin shimmied close and pinned her to the door. He had the same chin and light brown eyes as Jack and his brothers.

"Hello Zoe." His voice was gravelly. "I'm sorry for the forced introduction, but it seems my cousin has been hogging you all to himself."

Fresh fear seized her as she realized the man was Kyle. What had she been thinking leaving the party alone? She tried to push him away with her shoulder, but he was massive.

"Let me go!" Her heart drummed in her ears.

"It's not that simple." He snickered and rubbed a large bulge under the zipper of his pants. His eyes took on a light of a man possessed. "Fight me, witch."

"Jack said you're already mated." She flinched when his hand skimmed up her leg. "What do you need me for?"

"More is always better, especially when it belongs to Jack." His fingers latched onto her thigh, tightly. "The girl is just a distraction until I get my real prize."

He grabbed for her breasts but she bunched up and kneed him in the chest. The impact barely winded him. He chuckled and pulled her into his lap, forcing his mouth over hers. His breath was beyond foul. She gagged and bit his lip.

"You bitch!" He put a hand to a drip of blood running down his chin. His eyes grew even colder than before. "He hasn't fucked you, so I will."

New fear seared her brain. "I won't fight you."

"You already are." He leered and licked the blood off his fingers.

His heavy frame prevented her from squirming, but the second she broke free, she would scratch his eyes out.

"Trust me you'll be begging me for more before the night is through." He nestled his nose against her neck and inhaled deeply.

"Never." With every ounce of strength she had left, she brought her forehead down hard against his nose. She felt cartilage crunch, and blood sprayed.

"You'll mate with me or you'll wish you'd never been born." His fingers tangled in her hair and he yanked her head back. "Not all warlocks are pussy-whipped like Jack. Some of us know how to get what we want."

The car swerved into a lot next to a dilapidated building. The word '*Nudies*' lit the fog in red neon, along with '*Coors*' and '*Bud Light*.'

Kyle leaned over and inhaled through his nose, as if snorting cocaine.

He tore open her shirt and grabbed her breast, pinching hard.

Rage blurred her vision. Zoe leaned back and zapped a bolt of energy towards him.

He sucked in his breath and his eyes dilated.

"Keep it coming, witch."

The door opened and he dragged her by the hair out of the car.

Her scalp burned as she raced to keep pace. The sticky beer-soaked floor was actually a relief when he threw her down. She turned and her breath caught in her throat.

Finger-gun-man was standing in the corner. Her mind whirred but nothing made sense. Why would her stalker be here at the shore with Jack's cousin? He gazed at her, his expression giving nothing away. Then the corners of his lips drew up in a sickly grin.

Men gathered near. They leered at her with cold, emotionless eyes.

Kyle yanked her over to a pool table and slammed her face into the green felt. The wooden bumpers bruised her ribs when he pressed his weight against her. She tightened her lips, not giving him the satisfaction of crying out.

"C'mon witch, give it to me." His belt buckle clinked, his fly zipped, and he zapped her with sick, nauseating energy.

Her head pounded and beads of sweat rolled down the side of her face. She stretched to the center of the table and curled her fingers around a pool cue. She'd pierce his brains through the eye and watch them spew out his ears.

"Release her," a thickly accented voice demanded. Finger-gun-man. "She's mine."

She turned to look over her right shoulder, too frightened to watch, too frightened not to.

"That wasn't our agreement," Kyle bit out.

"I lied." The man shrugged, and with a burst of energy, pushed Kyle halfway across the room.

Screaming, Kyle raised his arm and sent a fiery ball into the chest of his nemesis. Finger-gun-man laughed with a kind of grunt. Lightning fast, a streak of black bolted across the room and Kyle was thrown to the floor. He rocked in a fetal position and wailed.

"Be happy I want your business or you would be dead." Finger-gun-man turned to Zoe with that same smile that had haunted her for weeks. He slowly unzipped the fly of his designer suit.

The fear she had felt when Kyle had held her down was nothing compared to what she felt now.

"You've managed to unlock your powers." His eyes twinkled and he licked his lips hungrily. "Good."

"Get away from me." Her voice was a rasp.

He slapped her so hard her ears pounded. "Fight me, witch."

Ignoring every instinct to the opposite, she lay limp.

He cursed, threw her to the floor, and stomped a shoe between her breasts. A billion shards of pain emanated from that one point. She screamed and prayed for relief.

The edges of her vision darkened, and she was about to surrender to unconsciousness when static electricity sparked her arm hairs. Electrons flowed to her, inside her, and more joined until they overflowed. She thought she'd spontaneously combusted when an angry vortex zoomed out of her body. It spun sparks and gathered papers, trash, and empty beer bottles into its center core. It crackled as glass splattered. She willed it towards finger-gun-man who had already backed away towards Kyle.

"Zoe. No." Was that Jack shouting? *Where the hell had he come from?* Without her concentration, the vortex fell apart and crashed to the floor.

Jack had a shotgun aimed squarely between finger-gun-man's eyes. Josh, Jase, and his dad carried equally menacing weapons with long barrels pointed in different directions.

"One wrong move and I'll castrate you," Jack said. The muscles in his shoulder and neck bunched.

Zoe scrambled off the floor, held her shirt closed as best she could, and ran towards the door. Jack grabbed her arm and shoved her behind him.

"It doesn't matter Jack," Kyle screeched from the floor. "He's more powerful than you. He'll have her. You'll see."

Finger-gun-man gave Kyle a fierce scowl.

Jack covered the door and whistled to his brothers. With their fingers resting against the triggers, each slowly inched away. Jack never took his eyes off finger-gun-man as he eased out of the bar.

He motioned to Zoe. "Get in the car."

"Jack–"

"*Get-In-The-Car.*"

* * *

Jack's Neanderthal brain hovered at the surface, barely tethered. She'd summoned a vortex. If he hadn't arrived when he did, there would have been no stopping the foreplay. And that was one duel he would've lost.

"Are you mad at me?" All innocence and angels, she blinked at him. *Damn her.* She was shivering despite the warm evening. Good. She should be scared.

Without a word, he grabbed his leather jacket from the backseat and placed it on her legs. He didn't trust himself to answer her.

They pulled up to his house and he put the gear in park, then got out of the car. He slammed the door so hard that a cat yowled and darted across the street.

"Who was that warlock? What are you up to?" he bit out through clenched teeth.

"Are you serious?"

"Stop playing games, Zoe."

"Oh my God, you are! *You* tell me who he was." Tears glittered in her eyes, and her hands fisted at her side. "You think I wanted this? Look at my face. My wrists. My clothes. Damn it, Jack, what is *wrong* with you? I was kidnapped and almost raped."

Zoe swiped angrily at the tears that ran down her cheeks and dashed up the stairs of the Victorian mansion.

Raped? Fuck. He'd been so focused on what he had almost lost, that he had barely noticed her appearance. Shit, he could be such an asshole. He started to follow after her, but his brothers and father arrived. The men's faces were drawn down in deep scowls as they got out of their vehicles.

Shit, there was no hiding Zoe's secret any longer.

Jack started to speak, but his father put a hand up, stopping him.

They made their way to the backyard, silently. His mom and sisters waited there along with Olivia. The rest of the crowd had cleared out. It was obvious by the women's expressions that someone had already informed them about what had happened.

Olivia stepped forward. "Where's Zoe?"

"In the house." Jack rubbed the back of his neck. "Can you see to her?"

She nodded, squeezed his hand in passing, then sprinted towards the yellow light of the kitchen. When the door opened, he swore he could hear Zoe's sobs.

He had to go to her. Fix things. A clap of thunder stopped him in his tracks.

"What's going on?" His father poured a finger of scotch and took a gulp. He filled another, added ice, and handed it to Jack.

"Kyle kidnapped her."

"I got that much, son." His father stared without blinking and swished the gold liquid in his glass.

Jack glanced up at the light that went on in Zoe's bedroom. Olivia's profile was dark against the shade. He should be up there, not down here under the inquisition. Damn it, he wasn't a kid anymore.

The ever-blabber-mouth Kathy spilled the beans. "She's not trained. Clueless. Adopted. And part healer. Jack oathed with her before he knew anything about her."

The thunder went to a rumble, the wind died, and the air was thick enough to pour into a glass.

Jack scratched at his scruff and stared into the astonished faces of his family. He unclenched his teeth so his jaw would stop ticking.

"You oathed with a complete stranger?" His father's all-knowing eyes lost nothing.

"Yes." *But she doesn't want me.* Jack sat down at a table and white-knuckled his glass.

"What aren't you telling us?" His father poured another drink, and gave Kathy a look that indicated she wasn't to speak.

His mom, dad, Kathy and brothers watched him. Jack shifted uncomfortably under their scrutiny.

"Last night, I was patrolling the bars with Stan and Josh. Looking for underage mating. I got hit with an assassin's energy. God-almighty powerful. Thought I'd bought it. Olivia left Zoe in charge. She healed me, but she's warring. She must be some kind of half-breed."

His mother did a sign for warding off evil.

"Who was the man with the accent?" Josh paced and felt for a pack of cigarettes in his shirt pocket.

Jack wasn't going to remind him that he'd quit years ago. "I don't know."

"But you suspect?" Kathy said, crossing her arms.

Oh yeah, he suspected. He suspected that Zoe had a secret lover. Someone that cared enough to follow her to the shore. Someone who was going to claim her as his own unless Jack convinced her otherwise.

"I think she knows him." There'd been an undeniable flash of recognition in her face. And she'd been willing to fight him. Jack cringed at the thought. If he hadn't stopped her, the night would have gone a hell of a lot worse.

"I'll make coffee." His mom walked by him and squeezed him on the shoulders. Kathy followed.

His father stared out at the crashing waves, then turned to Jack. "So you think you can mate with this *part-healer*?"

Jack ignored the insulting tone, stood, and met his father's icy stare. "I'm counting on it, sir."

"Then go upstairs and fix this, son. Take her before someone else does."

His father was right. But it was easier said than done. There was too much at stake, and he wasn't even sure the woman liked him, let alone wanted him for a mate.

Upstairs, he tapped on the bedroom door. He could hear the old shower humming from the bedroom bathroom.

Olivia opened the door and slipped out of the bedroom. She gave him a quick hug, then pulled back shaking her head.

"How is she?" Jack asked.

"Pretty shaken up. Stay out here until she invites you in. She needs to feel in control." Liv patted his arm. "Don't fuck this up any more than you already have."

Jack sat down on the floor and rested the back of his head on the doorframe. Downstairs, he could hear his family arguing. Eventually everyone left, but the shower continued to hum, barely drowning out Zoe's sobs.

Nearly a half hour later, the shower finally turned off and he heard the bathroom door scrape open.

He stood and knocked softly. "Open up, Zoe, I need to talk to you."

"Leave me alone."

Jack paced. *Don't screw up. Take her before someone else does.* How the hell was he supposed to do both? She wasn't prepared to mate with him, and even if she was, he doubted she wanted to after tonight.

He took a deep breath, placed his forehead on the door and tried again. "Tell me what happened."

Her footsteps crossed the room, but the door remained closed. He could hear her uneven breathing and soft sniffles.

"Zoe, talk to me."

A heavy slap sounded on the other side of the door and he jumped.

"You want to know what happened?" Her voice rose with each word she spoke, anger laced with fear. "I took a walk and got abducted by your drugged up cousin. While he had me pinned to a table, the stalker guy oathed with me." Her voice shook, and a small sob sounded behind the door. "Now you know and can go away–I'm going home."

"Stalker? What stalker?" He pounded on the heavy oak. "Open the damn door."

"I'm done being a pawn for oversexed warlocks. Go away. I'm not *mating* with anyone." She spit out the word like a curse.

"Angel, what do you need?" He placed his hands on both sides of the doorframe and closed his eyes. How was he ever going to make this right?

"Besides getting out of here?" Her voice lowered so that he could barely hear her words. "Ice. My face hurts like hell."

Jack raced into the kitchen and grabbed a bag of peas out of the freezer, then bounded back up the stairs. "I have something for your face. Open the door, Zoe."

The key rattled a couple of times, and she cracked a tiny opening and stared down at the handle with furrowed brows. "It wasn't locked."

His gut wrenched at the puffy welts on her cheek and the swollen eye that stared through the slit. The baggy sweatshirt and sweatpants made her look young, vulnerable. He ached to gather her into his arms until all the ugly was gone, but he would let her make that first move.

"I'm taking you down to the police station so you can press charges." He handed her the peas.

"A slap on the wrist for them and severe embarrassment for me?" She placed the makeshift ice pack on her swollen face. "I don't think so. Besides, I thought this behavior was normal for you guys."

Jack held back the curse forming on his lips. "The woman has to be willing. He tried to rape you."

"I wasn't willing the other night with you."

"That's not fair. I didn't know that you didn't know the rules. I thought you were willing. Besides, you said you wanted me. Don't you dare compare me to him."

"I know." She opened the door wider.

He scrubbed his fingers through his hair. "I'm so sorry about how I acted in the car. I thought you were going to mate with him."

"Why would you think that? They're foul beyond words." She shut her eyes and hid her face behind the frozen bag, then cringed and pulled it off. "It hurts when I do that."

He placed his hand gently over hers and placed the peas back over her eye.

"You were going to share yourself. I saw your vortex." He tried to keep his tone soft, gentle. Still, the words came out harsher than he'd intended.

"I didn't want him. He hit me. Tried to force me to fight." Zoe's hand shook.

"I know that now. I screwed up." He tilted her chin with his thumb and forced her to look at him. "Forgive me?"

"Yes." She fell into him, tiny shakes amplifying to a crescendo of full-bodied sobs. Words of anguish poured out like an awful crossword puzzle. He tried to make sense of it. Who was finger-gun-man? What awful nightmare was she reliving? Some words sounded like tonight but some held the weight of an older issue. In between tormented cries, her body struggled to rasp in air.

He lifted her in his arms and carried her to the bed, laying down beside her. His throat tightened and his eyes watered while he listened to her litany. Finally, her sobbing turned into little hiccups. What nightmare had this woman lived through?

"It's going to be all right. I won't let them hurt you again." He brushed her damp hair away from her tear-stained cheek.

She reached up wide-eyed and touched where he hadn't been able to hold back a tear. What had this woman done to him? He was supposed to convince her to mate with him and save his family for another generation, not cry for her.

Jack took her hand away from his face and kissed her fingertips. "I think there's a lot going on in that head of yours. Who was the warlock, Zoe?"

"I don't want to talk about it now." She wrapped her arm around him, while they lay side to side, and clung to him like a lifeline.

He captured her gaze. She was so beautiful, even all puffy and red.

Her eyes focused on his mouth and she inched forward.

"Zoe." He lowered his lips and brushed the top of hers. He could do this. Hold back the mating. For her, he could do anything. He kissed her forehead, then the tip of her nose. He needed her to understand how much he cared. That's what she needed—to feel safe.

She opened her eyes, dark and dilated, and he moaned. He tried to move away but she reached behind his head, tangled her fingers in his hair, and rested her plush lips upon his. He tried to notch his attraction down. This was all about her. About comfort. Not sex. Her mouth moved on his and he shared a chaste close-mouthed kiss. The sweetness mixed with the solstice lust had to be the best and worst torture ever.

"I have to leave now." He touched a lock of hair that had fallen into her eyes.

"Don't go."

Goosebumps shot down his spine and blood rushed to his cock. Her lips pressed against his. When he gasped, her tongue raked across his teeth, then pushed into his mouth.

His balls tightened painfully, the tormenting ache increasing. Her hips jerked towards him, begging for more. He clenched his teeth, but he couldn't hold back the groan that rumbled from his chest.

Around them, the air electrified.

God help him, he couldn't let her go. But he needed to get out of there before he destroyed them both. She wasn't strong enough to fight him, especially not after tonight.

"Jack," she moaned, when he drew back from the kiss.

He let his lips linger on hers a moment longer, then gritted his teeth, and unlocked his arms from around her.

"Get some rest," he said from the door. They'd both need their strength for what he had planned for them tomorrow.

Chapter 12

With coffee in one hand, Zoe tiptoed out onto the old wraparound porch and sunk into a cushioned wicker chair. It creaked into the silence with a warm welcome. Beyond the dunes, gulls soared and screeched over the muted thundering of the waves. Down at the end of the block, the sun poked its head between the tall houses and long blue shadows striped the quiet street.

She sucked in the energy surrounding her. It was so good and so right, and now she knew why. She was a witch. The elements were her balm. She stood, facing the ocean, and closed her eyes. The beach, the wind, and the water soothed her soul as bits of thoughts darted in and out.

What was she going to do about Jack? He didn't love her and she couldn't blame him. They'd just met. No doubt the sex would be mind-blowing, but there were all those screwed up rules.

There was an awful lot on the negative side of the balance sheet.

And yet, he'd come for her last night. No one had ever rescued her before.

The old screen door cracked open. Balancing an overly full mug, Jack hooked a foot so the door wouldn't slam. He sat down and frowned into the sun.

"What're you doing out here alone? Until we figure this thing out, you need to be guarded. Always." He downed his coffee like a sports drink and scowled.

"Good morning to you too." She gave a small, almost silent snort and leaned on the railing, coffee cup in hand.

"Sorry. Rough night sleeping," Jack said, his tone low. "You said last night that Kyle tried to..." His lips drew up in a sneer. "Force himself on you."

Zoe swallowed hard and nodded.

"If Kyle tried to mate with you, then he didn't find a woman to augment his powers." He stretched his legs in front of him and tilted his head back, eyes closed. When he opened them again, his expression was hard, unreadable. "If he wants to dual, I'll win, just like last time. We don't have to have sex this solstice. Understand?"

A wave of disappointment flooded through her. Was he serious?

"What about the other guy? The one with the accent–"

"I don't know." He stared off into the distance. His knuckles whitened around his coffee mug. "I have a team working to identify him."

"When he got close to me last night, he smelled of the same evil that almost killed you." She pulled her phone out of her pocket and went to the picture she'd captured of the stalker on the subway. "I didn't tell you. He's been following me for weeks."

Jack took her phone and snarled at the photo.

"You should have told me about him. Did you know he was down at the shore?" He handed her phone back. His dark eyes sparked with anger.

She nodded and chewed on her lip.

"How long?" His voice was clipped.

"I saw him yesterday morning. When you made me promise to come with you." She placed her coffee cup on the bannister and turned back to the ocean. The last thing she needed this morning was another lecture from him.

The swing creaked when Jack stood.

"I don't get you Zoe. It's like you walk into danger eyes wide open. That's really screwed up." He paced the porch, his expression darkening with every step.

Suddenly his hands were on her. His fingers curled around her upper arm and he jerked her to him. The soft brown of his eyes darkened, shining with need. Zoe swallowed hard.

"I'm putting a twenty-four-seven protection around you. I won't let anyone else claim you. You're mine." His voice was hoarse, his breath tickling her cheek. "Understand?"

"Yes," she whispered. *His?* The thought both excited and terrified her.

"Good." He released her abruptly and stormed back into the house.

Zoe let out the shaky breath she had been holding. There were two choices. Run or stay and fight.

Would either option ever make her happy?

Dealing with Jack wouldn't be easy, but if they could learn to work around their insane physical chemistry, they could help each other. Maybe even learn to care, to love. Zoe squashed the thought immediately. Jack had made it clear that mating wasn't about love.

A gull landed on the railing a few feet from her, squawked, then flew off.

If she ran, finger-gun-man would still be after her. With Jack, she was safe. His family would be hers. Finally, she would belong somewhere, to someone. But if that was ever going to happen, she needed to learn how to control her powers.

Air. That was the element that Kathy had told her she was to call upon. The basic element that governed her powers. Zoe lifted her palms and focused her thoughts and energy. A small vortex appeared, pinks and purples danced in her hands like a mini-tornado.

A small laugh escaped Zoe's lips and the vortex went spinning across the lawn, hitting the neighbors' mailbox. Metal and wood splintered and popped.

"Shit." Zoe clenched her fists and stopped the flow of energy. She still had a lot to learn if she was ever going to fight Jack and not kill them both, but for the first time, hope blossomed in her chest.

Zoe knew what she had to do.

She would stay and fight.

Chapter 13

Zoe moaned, and rubbed her sore, stiff muscles. She closed her eyes and let the warm spray of water gently wash away the stress of the day. She'd spent the entire day working with Jack's sister. Fear, mixed with sexual frustration was a good motivator, and by mid-afternoon, she had started to feel a bit more confident that she might actually live to see her next birthday.

Now, as day turned to night she actually had hope that she could be the mate Jack believed her to be.

Smiling, she turned off the shower and reached for a towel. A couple more days and she would be able to fight him, then they'd have nothing to fear. Jack could draw upon her powers and protect them both.

She dried herself off and placed the wet towel in the laundry bin. As she turned around to grab fresh clothes from the closet, the door to her bedroom swung open. Surprised by the sudden invasion, she let out a small gasp.

"I made pasta, if you're–" Jack froze in the doorway, his lips parted and eyes went wide, then darkened.

For a split second, she swore her heart stopped, just before it began pounding like a jackhammer in her chest. A hard rush of adrenaline pumped through her veins. Never in her life had she so willingly exposed her body to a man, but there was no shame standing in front of him, only undeniable need.

He inched towards her, his gaze devouring her body. His eyes gleamed with a wicked, sensual hunger that had her aching for his touch.

Desire and fear flashed through her. She didn't move. Couldn't. She was trapped by an overwhelming need to be with him. To mate–become one.

He didn't touch her, though she swore his energy reached out and began caressing her skin, making her body shiver in response. She wanted him more than she'd ever wanted anything.

"Fight me, witch, or get the fuck away. Far, far, away. Run. Now." His voice was a harsh, broken whisper. He clenched and unclenched his fists, and the small knot on his jaw twitched.

Every cell in her body screamed to make love, but another even stronger desire took precedence.

It was time to fight for what she wanted.

"I'll fight." She licked her lips and jutted her chin. "For you, I'll fight."

He inhaled sharply and took another step closer. Close enough that she could feel the warmth of his body, the intoxicating energy that flowed around him. He gripped her hips, pulling her hard against him. The tips of her breasts tightened as they brushed against the rough material of his shirt. Adrenaline surged, racing through her.

"If we start this–"

"I know." She placed her hands on his chest. The need for his touch overpowered all rational thought. "I'm ready."

His hand slid slowly over the curve of her breast, and his gaze locked on her, sending flares of exquisite pleasure racing across her skin. His head dipped towards her, capturing her mouth with a kiss. This time nothing was held back.

Her hands were in his hair, pulling her to him, desperate for more. His tongue met hers. Licking. Stroking. Caressing. His kiss was pure energy. She shivered and arched towards him.

His body exuded his essence in a wild electric current that surrounded them both.

She was on fire. Ecstasy laced with lust took over every rational thought.

"Fight me," he growled against her lips.

She whimpered when he pulled back. She conjured a tennis-sized ball of energy and thrust it into his midsection. He didn't even flinch.

"That's not going to do it, Zoe. Don't toy with me. I'm hungry. I need you. All of you."

He placed a palm blast just below her belly and she gasped in pain and pleasure. Damp heat spilled between her thighs.

She inhaled deeply and gathered the electrons around her, then threw a blast into his chest.

Wind and energy blew around them. A photo fell off the wall and crashed to the floor. The curtains blew and tangled as the wind picked up.

"Holy fuck." Jack stepped back with a shocked expression and she laughed. He paused with a little grin. "Oh, you are *so* going to pay for that."

He strode over, cupped her breast and his heat poured into her. The energy was like a magnet. Her core opened wide for him, calling to his thickness to end the madness. She throbbed so badly it was hard to stand.

"Do you want me, Zoe?" Jack smiled arrogantly, his eyes blazing and dark.

"Yes," she whimpered. More than she had ever thought possible.

"Then stop holding back." He kicked his power up to full and sent a searing bolt straight into her core.

She stumbled back. Heat infused her body, an inferno of sensation that completely overwhelmed her. She gasped for air.

"Fight me, Zoe." His voice stroked over her senses. He pulled his shirt over his head and tossed it to the floor.

He formed a perfectly round ball of fire, and tossed it at her. It exploded over her body.

How could she fight him when every nerve ending in her body screamed for more?

She sucked his electrons into her, and covered them with her own. In her mind's eye, she pictured how she would sink onto his beautiful shaft. How he would fill her, stretch her, bring her the release she so desperately yearned for. Her thighs clenched, and she could feel the throbbing need in her clit. She took the emotion, the desire, the hunger, and manifested it into a vortex. It left her body and grew to encompass him completely.

Jack's eyes closed and he groaned as the huge violet spinning body of energy encircled him. His head arched back and the muscles in his shoulder and neck tensed. Her name left his lips in a soft growl.

She reached her hands through the energy and caressed his body. She'd trapped him. A sense of power surged through her. She had full control. She placed her hands on his muscular chest and sent another surge of energy through him. His muscles bunched and rippled and she felt his heartbeat racing under her palms.

"Release me," he growled, his breathing rapid, rough.

Her lips quirked. *Not yet.* Knowing she had authority over his body, was both empowering and erotic.

"I want to touch you." She reached for his belt, unbuckling it. "Taste you."

Her fingers flicked the button of his jeans. His cock strained against the fabric. She tucked her fingers into the waistband of his boxer briefs, and his hips jerked when her fingers brushed against his engorged head.

"Zoe," he breathed out harshly. The blaze of lust in his eyes seared her.

She eased the material over his erection. His cock was long and thick, the heavy crown engorged. She wrapped her fingers around the swollen flesh and knelt in front of him. The power was hers. She could take and give what she wanted.

She looked up at him and licked her lips.

"You're not playing fair." Hunger flared in his eyes.

"You should have explained the rules better." She chuckled and held the base of his cock in one hand, and cupped his balls in the other. She rubbed the swollen head against her tongue, her lips, and licked the bead that formed at the tip. "Mmmm."

"Holy hell." A rumble echoed from his chest.

She caressed the engorged crest, then took him further into her mouth. He hissed when her tongue stroked the underside of his head.

"You've undone me, Zoe," he panted, his body rigid, his face contorted in blissful agony. "Stop. Please. I am going to come too soon."

She'd been forewarned that this was the final test. He had to verbally concede that she had trapped him. She flicked her tongue.

"I win."

"No more. Release me." His eyes were dark with lust. "You win. I'm yours."

Instead of releasing the vortex, she stepped into it with him and gave up all control. She needed him more.

His lips covered hers and his tongue swept into her mouth. She inhaled his scent, tasted his kiss, took everything he gave her.

The hot flesh of his erection pressed into her stomach. His hands gripped her hips and jerked her closer. Her knees weakened, and the sensitive flesh of her sex throbbed.

"Jack," she whispered his name with an edge of desperation.

The rough pad of his finger slid across her clit, and she jolted in response. His fingers stroked the sensitive flesh, parted the folds, and pushed into the depths, sending an ecstatic rush of sensations surging through her.

Whimpering in pleasure, she begged, "Don't stop."

"Now *you* yield, witch." He raked his teeth over her neck, while his palms slipped up her belly to cup her breasts.

She gasped and felt herself sinking into him.

"You know I already have."

Power coiled through him. Roughly, he hauled her to the bed. Her back met the mattress and he positioned himself above her. He spread her thighs wider with his knees. She curled her hands over his broad shoulders, feeling the muscles clench and tighten under her palms.

He stilled above her. The thick head of his cock nudged the swollen folds.

Amidst the addictive hunger, there was something more. Something Zoe didn't want to speculate on. For a moment, apprehension edged at her arousal.

"Say it, Zoe. Say you're mine."

It was a claiming.

He was claiming her.

And she desperately wanted to belong.

"I'm yours," she whispered.

He thrust into her, working himself deeper, his gaze locked with hers. She gasped and gripped his shoulders tighter. He eased back, then pushed inside her again, slowly, deeply. He filled her perfectly.

"Mine," he growled. "My mate."

"Yes." She was fighting to breathe. Fighting to make sense of the sensations tearing through her.

His hips jerked hard, burying himself further inside of her.

"You need to say it back to me, angel."

"My mate," she whimpered, feeling a new surge of energy pulsating through her body. A brilliant array of color, pleasure, and sensations vibrated through her. For a brief, intense moment, she felt as if her body and soul merged with his, and her senses exploded with the pleasure of it.

His cock throbbed inside her, thick and hard, stretching the sensitive tissue. Electric pulses began to race through her body.

Jack's jaw clenched, fighting for control. He pulled back, then slammed in harder and deeper, impaling her with swift, hard strokes.

She dug her nails into his shoulders and gasped. Her vision darkened as she cried out with her release. The pleasure broke her. Every neuron in her body seemed to explode in ecstasy.

The vortex burst, sending violent waves of energy ricocheting off the walls. She heard Jack's shout, felt the overpowering pleasure of his release pulsating inside her.

Closing her eyes, Zoe held onto him and knew nothing would ever be the same again.

She was lost to him.

Chapter 14

It was a long time before Jack found reality. Zoe rested on his chest and his hand caressed the smooth skin of her back. So soft, so feminine, so perfect. He actually uttered a small prayer of thanks to the Goddess who watched over them, something he seldom did. What had he done to deserve her? His wildest fantasies hadn't come close to what he'd just experienced.

When she stirred, he whispered into her ear, "Zoe."

He wanted to say more, but any words would lessen what they shared.

She had changed him. It was more than the new power surging through his veins. More than the mating. There was a sense of rightness that he'd never felt before.

Her eyes were half closed and she looked up at him dreamily. Even though she was his for life, damned if he didn't want her again.

"We did it," she said softly.

"We did." He searched her eyes and felt a twinge of guilt. "Do you have any regrets?"

She closed her eyes briefly, then looked at him with wide, trusting eyes. "No."

Jack exhaled. He hadn't even realized he'd been holding his breath.

She gave him the sweetest little smile and put her hand to his chest.

He wondered how many men had shared her body. It bothered him to think of her with anyone else. Neanderthal as it was. She wasn't a virgin, but she was tight as hell.

"How long has it been?"

"Hmm?" Zoe ran her fingers along his abs, and zapped him lightly with energy. He wasn't even sure she knew she was doing it.

"How long since you last had sex? You were so tight, so mine." Jack turned onto his side and blew a cool blast of air on her sweat-damp skin. Goosebumps formed. Her eyes widened and dilated for him. She licked her lips and waited for his kiss. He touched his lips gently to hers. "How long?"

"What does it matter?" She arched into him and wrapped her legs around his waist.

"It matters to me." Jack nipped at the sensitive skin along her neck. She would answer his question now or in just a few minutes screaming out his name. His hand covered her taunt nipples and he rolled them between his fingers, then squeezed. She responded with a moan.

"It's been years." She rolled on top of him, her legs straddling his waist, hands on either side of his head. "You're not the only one who gave up. I never got anything from it. I thought maybe I was broken. The big 'O' never happened during sex. Seriously. I had to resort to something with a battery."

He stared into her face, thinking she was pulling his leg, but her expression was guileless. He moaned her name and pulled her down to him.

They made love again, but this time he played with her with gentle magic and touches. He needed her to know, to understand, all the sides of mating. Every place he explored and shared his power, she responded fully to him. It would take him years to find which places she liked best.

She was an eager learner and damn fine at turning the tables on him. It wasn't long before they were lying, panting, completely sated.

Her cheeks were flushed and her lips swollen. There were a few bruises starting to show on her arms where he'd grabbed her too tightly.

"Did I hurt you?"

"No. Did I hurt you?" She smiled, raised his arm, and pointed out a few scratches on his side.

Jack kissed her nose and chuckled. "Not at all."

It was almost impossible to keep his hands from moving all over that smooth, soft, and sexy skin. Her stomach grumbled, and he frowned.

"C'mon." He sat up. "We haven't eaten or slept well for days. Let's go down and I'll make us some pasta. Then we'll come back up." He kissed her nose and winked. "I promise."

He moved off the bed and grabbed his jeans from the floor.

"You'll be able to beat them now, right?" She twisted on the bed and eyed him from head to toe.

"They won't have a chance." Jack opened his palm, visualized Zoe's vortex, and it appeared. A small fire burned within the green and violet wind. Damn. It felt so much like her, he might have to have her again before going downstairs. She opened her palm and it moved to her like a magnet. He'd never seen anything like that, either.

"Whoa, you got that from me? Cool. I can't wait to see what I got." She jumped up and down on the bed on her hands and knees, looking as excited as a kid on Christmas. She raised her hand.

"No." Jack pushed her hand down to her side. "Not in the house, and not without the city fire department parked out front. You're air, I'm fire. Together, the two are pretty potent."

"Fine."

"I mean it Zoe. You could blow up the entire house if you don't know how to control it." Jack tried to frown at her astonished face but couldn't. Not with that beautiful naked body, and her on her hands and knees. His mind went where any normal male mind would go.

"You go down first, I need a shower. I'll be right down." She made a cute little pout and slid her feet off the bed.

His eyes followed her perfect little ass into the shower. She was tan, lean, with runner's calves. No wonder they could lock so tightly around him. What harm would it do if he followed her in there? He sighed. As leader of the clan, he had a duty to inform the family that he had successfully mated. Not just mated, but brought a new line of power into their clan. That hadn't happened in centuries.

When he jogged down the stairs, he found his sister Kathy in the front hall, juggling the baby on one hip and a diaper bag on the other.

He frowned. "What are you doing here?"

"Dad called a meeting." She shoved the bag at him. "The rest of the family are on their way."

"Shit." So much for time alone with Zoe. He followed Kathy into the kitchen, and put the bag on a stool. "A phone call would have been nice."

"Josh has been calling for the last hour."

"I've been busy." He raised one eyebrow and smiled.

It took her a moment to register what he was implying, but when she finally did, she clapped a hand over her mouth and squeaked. His father and brothers came trampling through the door at the same moment.

"Jack did it," Kathy blurted out. "He mated with Zoe."

Jack tried to look casual, but he couldn't stop grinning from ear to ear. His father met his eyes, and returned the same grin.

"Good thing I brought this," Josh said, holding up a bottle of scotch. He clapped Jack on the back when he walked by. "I knew you could do it."

Jack huffed and took the snifter Josh handed him.

"You hoping for a boy or a girl?" Jase asked, grinning.

Josh slapped the younger of the Fialko brothers on the back of the head.

"What?" Jase asked, rubbing his hand over the spot.

"Doesn't matter," Jack whispered, glancing quickly at the doorway. "Don't mention that part to Zoe."

Josh's eyes widened. "What? She doesn't know? How is that even possible?"

"We didn't get the chance to talk about it."

Jase snorted and Josh whistled low.

"Anyways, let's not spook her just yet. It's been a rough few days for both of us. I've hardly had a chance to get to know her."

"Where is she?" Kathy asked, cradling the baby against her shoulder. Yolanda gave a tiny sigh and closed her eyes.

"Upstairs."

"You need to tell her," Kathy said, her lips pursed.

"Stop with the looks. I'll tell her. Right after we take care of Kyle and his new *friend*."

Chapter 15

"Remember, we're going to take Kyle someplace and get him cleaned up. Try not to hurt him." Jack met the eyes of each member of his clan. "Leave the foreigner to me. Everyone understand?"

They all nodded except for Stan who was distracted, texting. He hastily put the phone in his pocket when Jack walked over. "Sorry. You were saying?"

"We need to go get Kyle now. We'll get him into rehab. You okay with this?"

Stan frowned but didn't put up a protest. "He's probably at O'Malley's."

"Figures. South Philly." Jack fingered his service revolver. "You guys hang back a little. I'm not quite sure what Zoe's vortex will do for me in a real fight, and I don't want anyone getting hurt."

It took about an hour to get to the bar. They parked outside in the desolate corner parking lot. Abandoned construction walls of plywood hid the area from the view of nearby businesses. A few men hanging out in front of a check cashing station ducked inside, as did a few in front of a bodega. Within seconds, the place was deserted.

When he got out of his car, Stan strode over and held a cell phone out to him. "I think you'll want to see this."

"That's my phone," Jack frowned, an uneasy feeling gripping his gut.

Stan winced and looked away.

Jack took the phone and his blood went cold. It was a snapshot of Zoe, blindfolded, sitting in a small room with a gun to her head. Behind her, assorted boxes of alcohol were stacked high to the ceiling. His heart went into his throat and he saw nothing but red. He grabbed Stan by the neck. In his other hand, he lit a vortex two inches from the weasel's face.

"Where is she?" he gritted out through clenched teeth.

Before Stan could reply, a steel door screeched open. Kyle leaned against the frame, his dark hair matted, his jeans torn, and despite his enormous size, his cheeks and eyes were dark sunken holes.

"Best you put my brother down and come inside." Kyle laughed, sounding crazy as hell. He threw a blast at Jack, then made a large sweeping motion over the parking lot. "Everyone else stays outside."

The electric energy sizzled in Jack's midsection, but he was too angry to feel the pain.

"Let her go, and I'll let you live." Jack kept his voice calm, despite the rage and terror that tore through him.

His cousin had finally lost it. Even the blast felt drugged up. But it wasn't powerful, and again, it wasn't what had hit him and almost got him killed the other night.

"Let me help you with the rules of the game." Kyle sneered and fingered another ball of energy. "Page three hundred and one. If you win, *she dies.*"

Jack could barely contain the fury building inside him, the need to protect Zoe. But losing his cool wouldn't do either of them any good. He glanced at Josh with a raised eyebrow, indicating he was to stand by. His brother gave an almost imperceptible nod back.

Stan led him into the building, up the cracked wood stairs and into the bar. The room was torn apart, as if demolition had started years ago, but was then left abandoned.

Jack breathed in the stuffy air and tried to focus on Zoe's energy. Nothing. He couldn't sense her. All he got was a repugnant muddle of dark energy. There were at least twenty to thirty men in the building. He recognized most of them as his own clan members.

Fear nearly choked him. Zoe couldn't die. Not now. Not after what they'd shared.

He'd kill Kyle and his gang the minute he had the chance. How the hell had they got her out of the house? He should never have left her alone.

Stay calm, he reminded himself. If he killed either one, he might not find out where she was hidden.

"I want to talk to her." Jack leaned against what was left of an old bar, hiding how tightly he was wound.

"First, admit that I've outplayed you." Kyle, using plywood as a table, snorted something up his nose with a rolled bill.

"No, you haven't. I talk to her right now or I assume she is dead and take the next logical step." Jack spun a small fire-vortex in his left hand and started to take aim with a revolver in his right. A few of the gang members mumbled nervously among themselves and then left the room one by one.

"What the fuck." Kyle stared at the small tornado, eyes and mouth wide. "Relax, Jack. I'm just getting you all worked up."

He texted something into his phone, and a moment later, Jack's cell rang with the ring tone he had reserved for Zoe.

"Zoe?" He cringed at the panic he heard in his voice.

"Jack, I'm okay. I thought–"

The connection hung up. After a wave of relief washed over him, Jack focused on Kyle with a deadly calm. He was a dead man walking – he just didn't know to lie down yet.

In his peripheral vision, Jack picked up five or six men entering the room. A few he recognized. The young woman who Kyle had claimed he mated with came in behind them. Her long dark hair hung disheveled around her face. There were dark bruises under her eyes and along her exposed arms. She glanced at Jack and the air in his lungs left him. Up close he could tell that she was younger than he'd first thought. Barely thirteen if he had to guess. Fuck, what was Kyle thinking?

"Dealing in pedophilia now?" Jack snarled. "That's low, even for you."

"Fuck you, Jack!" Kyle glared at the girl, raised his hand like he was going to hit her, and snapped, "Get back to your room."

The girl's eyes widened and she scurried away. Kyle smirked and turned back to his makeshift table.

"As I was saying…" He snorted the white powder again, which seemed to allow him to regain some of his bravado. He was oblivious to the fact that these might be his last words. "If I lose, she dies. I get injured, she dies. Get the picture?"

He threw another blow to Jack's midsection. Jack easily deflected the energy and used the opportunity to back towards the exit. That had to be where they kept her.

"Uh-uh. No slipping away." Kyle picked up his phone and texted again. "Tonight you're going to step down as clan leader."

Kyle sent Jack another blast, this time more powerful, and Jack gritted his teeth.

"It won't do you any good, Kyle. We've already mated." He brought his palm up and created a small vortex.

"Don't care. She's still a hot piece of ass. Besides, I have a buyer, even if she's damaged goods."

Kyle started to text again and Jack felt the oncoming firestorm, like a déjà vu, milliseconds before it happened. Zoe. Holy shit, the place was going to detonate.

Jack enlarged the vortex still spinning in his hand, added shielding, and stepped into it.

In the blink of an eye, Jack was knocked flat against the far wall and the bar was engulfed in flames. The explosion left him stunned, partially deaf, and smelling of liquor and sulfur. When the smoke thinned a bit, he saw Zoe below, curled up in a little ball, hands over her head, face down. Beside her lay a blackened corpse, the flesh charred and still sizzling.

Jack's heart stopped.

He dropped down into the supply room and squatted next to her. Before he could find a pulse, she turned and put her face into his hand. She was alive. He held her close until he could feel her heartbeat against his.

"Zoe." He could barely speak his throat was so tight.

All signs indicated that a tornado laced with fire had blasted outward from her. Splinters of charred wood pierced through chairs and into the walls behind. Shards of colorful glass and human flesh were strewn everywhere in a horrifying mosaic. Large pieces of bone and skin fell off the wall with a splat and sizzle. Thank God he'd felt the storm coming.

Everything was on fire. He stood, grabbed her into his vortex, and ran like a madman out of the building, just as the building hit the flashpoint.

He put her down on the pavement, dropped the magic, and felt all over her body for injuries.

Ghostly pale, she just stared into the inferno, eyes vacant. Her body began to convulse. He held her tight until she pushed him away and buckled over. She retched onto the pavement. When she was finished, he pulled her back against him. She went limp, almost lifeless in his arms.

"What happened, Zoe?" He pushed her sweat-soaked hair off her forehead.

"When you left, I was in the kitchen." She stared down at her hands, brows furrowed as if trying to remember. "I heard a noise." She looked up at him and blinked. "It was Stan. I knew something was wrong. I tried to run, but he...he grabbed me....covered my mouth with something...then everything went black."

Un-fucking-believable. He was going to kill the bastard, if he wasn't dead already.

"When I woke up, finger-gun-man was there...he...he tried–" She squeezed her eyes shut and her lower lip trembled. "I panicked."

"It's over now." He rubbed at the goosebumps on her arms. Her skin was ice cold.

An old-fashioned fire whistle began honking every few seconds in the distance. Damn it. He had a lot to do before the firefighters and police showed up.

Zoe moaned from her seat on the curb and held her stomach.

An out of breath Josh sprinted to their spot on the pavement. "Thank God you got out in time. Either of you hurt?"

Jack shook his head. "Any injuries among our men?"

"Not sure. We're still counting heads. What the fuck happened in there?"

Jack raised his eyebrows and flashed his gaze towards his mate. Josh got his meaning and flinched.

"She could've killed us all."

Jack mentally agreed. Zoe was very powerful and very unskilled. A bad combination. He grimaced as a vision of fried body parts flashed across his brain.

"I'm sorry." Zoe shivered and let out a small whimper. "I didn't mean to hurt anyone."

"We'll fix it." Jack pulled her against his chest and gave Josh a hard look when he started to say something. They needed to get the situation under control. The last thing he wanted was for this to be leaked to the global court. He wouldn't see Zoe stand trial for something she had no control over.

Jack's men were scattered around the building, trying to help the injured, but most of those that could, were running away, disappearing into the side streets.

"I need to take care of a few things." Jack squeezed Zoe's hand, then stood as his brother Jase approached. A few of Kyle's gang wandered about in a daze, but they weren't the one man he was interested in. "Any sign of Stan?"

"Dead." Jase glanced at Zoe, his brows drawn tightly down. "He was downstairs."

Zoe shuddered and buried her face in her arms. He ached to comfort her, but his clan needed their leader.

"Anyone hurt from our men?"

Jase shook his head. "Nothing serious. Just some injuries from flying debris."

Jack turned his head to the sound of sirens in the distance.

The young girl that had been with Kyle sat on the curb, her arms wrapped tightly around her chest. Other than the bruises he'd seen earlier, she seemed unharmed. "Have you spoken with the girl?"

"Doesn't speak much English." Jase frowned and dragged his fingers through his disheveled hair. "Not sure what to do with her."

"Take her to mom and dad. She'll be safe with them until we figure out where she came from."

Jase gave a hard nod. "You need to go. Who knows what she'll say."

"We're going to need to cover this one up. Luckily it looks like something exploded. It shouldn't be too hard to reinforce the notion of some kind of meth lab. Kyle was into some bad shit. The local cops will see what they want to see. Just push their will a little in that direction."

"Got it." Josh nodded. "I think it would be best to say Stan was a casualty of the explosion. It would kill Aunt Jane and Uncle Bill to know what hand he played in this. They've lost two sons tonight."

"Agreed." Jack squatted next to his mate and placed his hand on her arm. "Zoe, we have to go now."

Her head snapped up, eyes wide. "What did you do to me?"

"We can talk about this when we get you somewhere safe." Jack took her elbows and lifted her to her feet.

"No." She pounded her fists on his chest, and began to shout, "I killed people. You did that to me."

Josh and Jase raised their eyebrows and walked away.

"Zoe, relax." He gripped her wrists so she couldn't hit him. "Everything is going to okay. We just need to get out of here before the emergency crews arrive."

The last of the flaming bar collapsed with a sickening crack, and a few more bottles of alcohol exploded.

"Nothing is okay." She pulled her arms free, then placed her forehead on his chest, sobbing. "What kind of power is that? I'm a...a fucking killing machine."

Jack let her rant and pulled a few strands of sticky hair out of her mouth. He'd tried to warn her, but even he was surprised at the extent of her power.

"Everyone is different when it comes to this kind of thing. The augmentation of power of our kind is very rare. It's only because you were so frightened that your energy came out like that."

"I could've killed you." She gave his chest another hard whack.

"Enough." He gripped both her wrists in one of his hands. "Half of your newfound power came from me. I felt it coming. You can't hurt me."

The lie sounded better than the truth. He tried to soothe her with his free hand by rubbing her shoulders. She shivered, and giant tears made streams of dirt along her cheeks before dripping onto his shirt.

"Time to get you home." Jack scooped her into his arms.

He placed her in the leather passenger seat of the dark sedan and shut the door. Immediately, she tucked her legs under her chin and curled up in a ball.

He took one last look at the burning building and shuddered.

What a fucking nightmare.

The sirens were getting louder. They pulled out of the parking lot, just as the rescue vehicles zoomed past them with alarms blaring.

Chapter 16

Jack breathed a discernible sigh of relief when they pulled up to the cottage and saw Olivia waiting for them. No doubt his brother had called her to let her know what happened.

Zoe hadn't said a word since he'd placed her in the car. She just stared out the window, with silent tears running down her face. He could sense the emotions warring inside her. Guilt, anger, and grief swam behind her eyes. Jack had never felt so completely helpless in his entire life.

He placed his hand on hers and she flinched.

Olivia rushed from the porch towards them, her eyes wide. "Josh called me. Are you all right?"

Zoe got out of the car, zombie-like, and fell into her cousin's arms. Her shoulders heaved as giant sobs shook her.

"Let's get you inside," Liv said. With her arm over Zoe's shoulder, she led her into the house.

He leaned against the car and exhaled. His own cousins were dead. Assholes or not, they were his family. Stan had been like a brother to him. Why he would turn against him was beyond Jack's reasoning.

What a cluster-fuck. He wiped his hand across his face. When he glanced at his fingers, they were covered in dust, tears and blood.

Breathing in deeply, he pushed off the car. Olivia met him at the door.

"Where is she?" His voice broke with pent-up emotion.

Olivia nodded at the bathroom door. "What the hell happened out there?"

He gave her a quick rundown of the night's events. "...she blew the place to bits. Fried Kyle, Stan, and a couple members of Kyle's gang. We got out just before the police arrived. Stan and Josh are covering."

Olivia's face twisted with grief. "Kyle was into some bad shit, but this is over-the-top, even for him. He wasn't that smart. Neither was Stan."

"No," Jack agreed. His fingers clenched and unclenched. He desperately needed to hit something right now.

"If it wasn't Kyle, then who's behind it?"

"I don't know his name but I'm going to find out." Jack suspected the man who had been stalking Zoe was involved in more ways than they had originally thought. He glanced at the bathroom door and grimaced. "We need to make sure she calms down and says nothing to anyone–witch or human."

Olivia nodded. "I'll go make some tea. She'll need something to help her sleep."

He knocked on the bathroom door.

"Go away," Zoe sobbed.

"Unlock the bathroom door and let me in." Jack kept his voice low, yet firm.

"Please, Jack, just go away. I want to be alone." Zoe started crying hysterically again. "It's because of you I'm a walking napalm bomb." Her breath hissed and she cried out, "Oh my God, I've got pieces of fried human flesh in my hair."

Jack couldn't take anymore. He cursed under his breath and kicked the bathroom door in. It felt damn good to break something.

Shocked, Zoe looked up at him, her head next to the toilet bowl.

He knelt down and wrapped his arms around her the best he could. "I'm so sorry. It's my fault."

"You're damn right it's your fault." Zoe pushed him away, stood and moved towards the shower.

Jack barely had time to react when the first bottle of shampoo flew across the room, hitting him square in the chest.

"How could you do this to me?" Next, she threw a huge bottle of conditioner at him, then soap, and then conjured a vortex as if to hit him. She shook it out of her hand as if it burned her skin. Her eyes widened and her voice rose. "I could've just blown up the house...and Olivia. You've made me into some kind of freaking monster. I just blew people into bits and they're in my hair."

Olivia hovered by the bathroom door. "Let me handle this for a while, okay?"

Jack nodded and went back to his pacing, while Olivia helped Zoe with her shower. She spoke softly and said all the soothing words that he'd never be able to say and it pissed him off. He should be the one comforting her.

When Olivia exited the bathroom, Jack raised his eyebrows in question. She frowned and shook her head.

"She's coming home with me." Olivia stepped in front of the door when he moved towards it.

"I'm not leaving her alone." Jack's heart fell, and panic seared his brain. He wasn't letting her go. She was his mate.

"Did you ever once think about the consequences of joining with her? What it might do to her?" Olivia crossed her arms over her chest and pursed her lips. "You're all set now. You got what you wanted. Power. Your clan. But at what cost?"

Olivia stopped talking when Zoe came out of the bathroom. Her eyes were puffy and swollen, her nose pink. She looked so vulnerable and lost that his chest physically constricted. He'd done this to her.

She glanced at him briefly, then started down the hall. He tried to reach out, but she pushed past him.

"Don't try to stop me."

"Zoe, we need to talk." He followed her when she walked upstairs to her bedroom. She started to shove her clothes into a duffle bag and he grabbed her arm to stop her. "I won't let you leave."

"You got what you needed." Tears glittered in her eyes and her shoulders slumped in defeat. "Now let me go."

"You belong with me." Jack dropped his hands to his side and clenched his fists to keep from going postal.

She spun on him, anger blazing in her eyes. "I killed people tonight."

Jack grimaced and took a step towards her, but she flinched away the moment he tried to touch her.

"I need some space. I gave you everything you wanted. We had some fucking incredible sex, you got to augment your powers, and your clan is safe. I wouldn't take any of that back. Really, I wouldn't."

"We're mated. That's for life, Zoe. I know you can feel that."

"Yeah, I feel it." She closed her eyes and breathed out hard. "But I can't live like this."

He sat down on the edge of the bed and dragged his hands over his face. "My life isn't always like this. Most of the time it's fairly normal."

"I don't belong in your world." She shook her head and glanced down at her hands. Her eyes squeezed shut and a tear slid down her cheek.

She started towards the door, and he caught her arm.

"There still might be someone out there threatening you. I won't lose you. I just found you." He pulled her against him.

"If you really want to make this work, then give me some space to adjust." She sighed and placed her forehead against his chest.

"How much space?"

"I don't know. Let me go back to New York, go to work."

He clenched his teeth, fear paralyzing him. Getting angry wasn't going to help.

"We're mated," he said again. "There's no walking away."

"But that's all it is. Nothing more." Zoe lifted her head and stared into his eyes.

She left the giant question mark hanging between them. Jack knew what she was looking for, but he wouldn't lie, at least not about that.

"It's enough," he said finally.

Zoe sighed. "Not for me."

Chapter 17

"No, absolutely not!" Jack's voice boomed into her dream.

She moaned and blinked her heavy lids, not wanting to wake up to reality. The morning sun cast a yellow haze in the small room, and the smell of fresh coffee wafted through the door. She'd let Jack convince her to stay the night, but today she would head back to New York.

For her own sanity, she had to.

Jack and Olivia continued to argue just outside her bedroom door.

"Be reasonable, you need to tell her, Jack." Olivia's voice sounded tired and strained.

"She'll find out soon enough. I just need some time."

"You're so pigheaded, I swear..."

Heavy footsteps bounded down the stairs until Zoe could no longer hear their conversation.

The front door opened and banged closed. Zoe raced to raise the bedroom window while the two continued their argument. Olivia had one hand on her hip and was pointing and shaking her index finger at Jack.

What was it he didn't want her to know?

Zoe cursed and ran down the stairs and out the door. The sharp stones split the skin on her bare feet and the brisk wind cut through her light t-shirt.

"I hate it when you guys do this. What are you two hiding from me, now?"

"Go upstairs and put some clothes on, Zoe. I'll be up in a minute." Jack didn't give her the satisfaction of meeting her angry gaze.

"No way, Fialko." She glanced down and realized she had run out of the house wearing only an oversized t-shirt. Damn it. She crossed her arms over her breasts. "I'm sick and tired of being kept in the dark. Tell me now."

"Fine. Can we talk in private?" He scowled at Olivia who nodded and stormed down out past the dunes.

Her flowing clothes and long red hair whipped around her in the early morning sunlight, creating the illusion of one very angry goddess. The waves from the ocean drummed and crashed with her every step.

She followed him back to the porch.

"Let's go inside." Jack's mouth was in a grim line and his jaw clenched. His tension matched the relentless crashing of the stormy ocean and the screeching of the gulls.

"No. Tell me now." She sat down on the swing and shivered.

"You're not even dressed." Jack placed his jacket over her bare legs.

She narrowed her eyes at him. "Now, Jack."

"I was going to tell you." He pulled off his sunglasses, revealing dark circles. "There just hasn't been a chance."

"You have your chance now." Zoe drank in his beautiful eyes, then looked down. Damn, her body responded to him, despite everything.

There was a long silence.

Jack exhaled slowly and knelt in front of her. He tucked his finger under her chin, and drew her eyes to meet his serious gaze. "Look at me, Zoe."

She did, and what she saw nearly gutted her. There was real fear in his eyes. How bad could it be?

"Just tell me," she whispered.

"When we mated, you got one other thing besides my power."

"What are talking about?" She licked her suddenly dry lips and eyed him nervously.

"You're pregnant, Zoe."

A hysterical laugh escaped her lips, but her smile fell when she realized he was being serious.

"It's not possible. We just had sex last night and I'm on the pill."

"Doesn't matter, angel. It's a mating thing." He gripped her hands.

She pulled away. "You *knew* this would happen and you didn't warn me?"

"I thought you understood. That you had read through all the rules. You recited that one back to me so well. I just assumed–"

"You assumed wrong." There was anger in her voice, but she felt numb from the inside out. Pregnant. Her. She wouldn't believe it if everything in her world weren't already so screwed up.

"Are you all right?" His voice quavered.

After everything they had gone through, this was the first time he'd sounded frightened, and that scared her more than anything.

"I don't know. I wouldn't have wanted your family falling into the hands of that drug-crazed creep. And I certainly didn't want you to die in a duel with finger-gun-man." She shook her head. "But a baby? I can barely take care of myself."

"You won't do anything..." His expression tightened and his face paled. "You're not alone in this. If you don't want it, my family will help raise the child."

"What kind of person do you think I am?" She gave him a horrified look and pulled her hands from his grip. She stood and began pacing the porch.

"I have everything you need. I'll take care of you both. Stay with me. Marry me."

She froze. *Marry him?*

"I barely even know you." She placed her palms on the railing and looked out at the beach. For a brief moment she let herself imagine a life with him, with their child. She squeezed her eyes shut and shook her head. It was foolishness and it would never work. They were too different, and he would never be able to give her what she really needed.

Her shoulders hunched and she breathed in through her nose. She needed to get out of this godforsaken town, and away from him, if she was ever going to have a clear thought again.

"Zoe, please–"

"I'm not going to move in with you, let alone marry you." She stared out at the ocean and spoke with as much stoicism as she could muster. "We had a couple of very intense days followed by mind-blowing incredible sex, but we're talking about real life here, not a magic-solstice-witchy moment in a Victorian beach house."

"You're wrong, Zoe." Jack gripped her shoulders and turned her so she could see the fury blazing in his eyes. She swore she could see real fire in the blackened centers. "We didn't fuck. We mated and we're going to have a baby and be a family. I may not know you very well, but Zoe, I feel you, here"–he banged on his chest–"constantly. I know you feel it too."

Of course she did. She felt him in a way that was overwhelming. He was there, constantly. Ever since she'd met him she couldn't get him out of her mind. But she couldn't tell him that. He already treated her like he owned her. Soon she would shrink to nothing against his constant ego and she would revert to nothing.

Men always wanted ownership, body and soul. It was just like how her father had owned her until she finally left home. Zoe wanted to be free. More than that, she wanted to be loved, unconditionally, not chained to a relationship through magic.

"This won't work." She shook her head.

"It will. Just give it time." Jack pulled her to him, and blasted her with a heat that warmed her very core.

He wasn't playing fair.

"Let me go." Zoe pushed weakly with both hands against his armor-like chest. "Haven't you done enough to me already?"

"I'll fix things." He held her tight. "Just give me the chance."

She sank her face against his chest. His scent drifted into her nostrils, making her knees go weak. Already her traitorous body recognized him as her own and lusted after him.

How was she ever going to find the strength to walk away?

* * *

Confused, hurt, and angry, Jack held Zoe against him, worried that she would slip from him if he gave her even the slightest chance. Why was she so damn adamant about running from him? He'd give her the world if she'd only give him the chance.

"Don't run from me, Zoe." He placed his hand over her abdomen. He could already sense another presence growing within her and it overwhelmed him. She needed to understand. Maybe he didn't love her, but it was damn close to it. He moved his hand to her chest, and shared his emotions with a pulse of energy. It left him out there, feeling vulnerable as hell.

"Jack?" She blinked up at him.

"That's what I feel for you angel."

"I can't think straight when I'm with you."

"Then don't think." He brushed his lips over hers. "Just feel."

He nipped at her lips and sent tiny waves of heat through his fingertips along her bare thigh. She kissed him then. More like, devoured him.

The energy between them was palatable. *Fuck, she felt so good.* Maybe everything was going to be all right after all.

"I don't want to live without you." He slowly put his hand over her heart and pulsed in his energy.

Her little gasp set him on fire.

"Look at me, angel." He placed her hand on his chest. "Feed me your lust, your power–*your everything*. I need it, sweetheart. I need to know you want to be mine. Like you did for me the first time."

Zoe opened her eyes, gazed into his, and tentatively gave him what he asked. Jack inhaled sharply as blood rushed to his cock.

She groaned into his mouth, and rubbed against the hard erection that pressed against the fly of his jeans. Damn if he didn't want to unzip it there, push her against the wall of the cottage, and take her.

"We're going inside. Now." He bent down, placed his arm under her knees and scooped her up.

She let out a little squeal, and he stopped her protest with a kiss.

They were both breathing hard when they reached her bedroom. Her face was flushed with desire as he placed her feet on the ground and let her slide down his body.

Hating the barrier of their clothes, he gripped the hem of her shirt and pulled it over her head. Her hands went to the buckle at his waist, and he groaned when her fingers brushed against his erection.

He cupped the back of her neck, knotting his fingers in her hair, and lowered his lips to hers. Her mouth parted for him. He devoured her, and she rose against him, straining for more. She met him with an intensity that matched his own.

It was like tasting wind and fire–an inferno of desire.

He clenched his teeth. His body was strung tight and his cock throbbed in agony. He needed to be inside her. Now.

She placed her hands on his chest, a wicked gleam in her eyes, and gave him a solid blast that sent him stumbling back against the bed.

He inhaled roughly.

She blasted him again. Fire and wind shot through him, straight to his balls, and he collapsed backwards on the bed, panting. She crawled on top of him and licked her lips.

"Fuck, you're beautiful." He barely contained the primal growl that rumbled in his chest as she blasted him with another surge of energy. Her essence swirled through him, and for a moment, he couldn't breathe.

Her eyes glittered with challenge. She wanted to play.

He chuckled, gripped her hips and flipped her on her back. She let out a small squeal of surprise, and he used that moment to conjure a large ball of sexually charged energy. He held it above her stomach. He smirked and lowered his mouth to her breast. He licked and nipped her hardened nipple.

"Tell me you want it, angel." He lowered the ball so that it sizzled and sparked just between her legs.

"Please," her weak cry was desperate.

He placed his palm between her thighs and let the energy flood through her. Her head tossed, and her hips rocked beneath his hand. He blew a cool breath over her taut nipple and her body convulsed with another spasm.

The sound of her cries overwhelmed his senses. There was no holding back. He lifted above her and pressed his cock against her swollen folds. She was warm, slick, and ready for him. He drove himself deep, filling her to capacity.

"More," she pleaded. She rocked her hips against his, driving him even deeper. Her fingers clawed at his hips, his back.

"Stay with me, Zoe." He put his hand on her chest and with another dose of energy, let her feel his want for her as he thrust hard and deep. She was his mate. Fully, completely. What more could any person want?

"Jack." She closed her eyes and gasped.

Her body tightened. He could feel her orgasm building. She clawed at the sheets, her head tilted back, and her body clenched and convulsed around him.

Holy Goddess. The sensation drove him over the edge.

Intense pleasure tore through him. Heat and wind whipped around them. With one final thrust, Jack shouted in ecstasy. The final burst of his release pulsed through his body and he collapsed above her.

His cock throbbed inside her, and he fought for breath, for sanity. He brushed his lips over her neck, then rolled on his back, bringing her with him.

"I can't live without you, angel," he said. "I can't let you go. Not part-time. Not anytime. We'll go back to New York and figure this whole thing out, together."

She gave him a noncommittal nod.

He played with a stand of her hair. "But I have to ask you drop the freelance hacking once we get back."

"How do you know about that?" she frowned.

"What good is it to have money if I can't spend it figuring out what you do for a living?" He chuckled and kissed her gently on her swollen lips.

"You've been investigating me?"

"You knew I was looking into your past." He stood and started to dress.

Her frown deepened. "That's different."

"Just promise me no more illegal activities."

"Fine." She sat up and pulled her knees under her chin. "But I'm not going to move in with you. Not yet. Nan said I could stay at her place until she gets back."

"We already discussed this." He shrugged his shirt on.

"No, you made your demands. I didn't agree to anything." She picked at a thread on the comforter, not meeting his eye. "I need some space to get used to everything."

"Who's Nan?" Jack sat down on the bed and put on his shoes. He'd ignore her comment for now. She'd move in with him whether she liked it or not, she just didn't know it yet.

"A friend." She bit her lip and looked out the window, her expression unreadable.

He moved closer and held her head gently to face his own, their noses touching.

"I thought we were good?" He searched her eyes for some kind of reasoning and reassurance.

"We are good. But I really don't know you, and I'm not ready to move in with you. Believe me when I say, you're not ready for me." She shook her head when he opened his mouth to speak. "And don't say it. I know you're my mate."

He muttered a curse under his breath and stood.

"I'm not disagreeing that when it comes to making love, nothing is even close, but we don't even know if we even like the same TV shows. Movies. Do you leave the seat up? Do you drink milk out of the carton? Will you use my toothbrush? What if we drive each other crazy?" She sighed and tucked her hair behind her ears. "We need to slow down."

"Kind of late for that," he muttered, trying not to sound angry.

"I gave you what you needed. Give me the same courtesy." She raised her voice a notch and he felt his temper start to snap.

Before he realized it, he was shouting. "What *do* you need, then?"

She stood up suddenly, naked and heated. Thunder broke in the distance, and a cool breeze blew through the window, causing the blinds to complain and the curtains to stir.

"Really?" she shouted back. "This is the first time you've asked. *That's* what I need, Jack. Someone who wants to know what *I* need." She opened a drawer and pulled out a bra and panties, then slipped them on. "So far, it's been all about you."

He lowered his voice "Have I fucked everything up that badly?"

"For you, it's easy. You call me your mate, we have sex and it's done. For me, I only know human relationships and how they work, or rather, maybe, mostly how they don't work. I can't trust your way. You have to admit, it's caused a lot of problems for me so far." She finished dressing and twisted her hair high on her head, securing it with an elastic. "My number is in your cell. We'll drive back to New York. I'll get settled at Nan's and then we can go out for dinner."

"Okay," he sighed. "What do you like to eat? I'll make reservations."

"Surprise me."

He had no comeback. Other than eggs, he had no idea what she liked, and just like that, she drove her point home. He turned, partly dejected and decidedly angry. He'd personally follow her to New York and then make some calls to have her watched. He wasn't going to lose her again.

Chapter 18

Ivar couldn't believe his good fortune. The couple had taken both cars to drive north. He pulled into the slow lane, directly beside the son-of-whore who had stolen his clan's vortex. When the traffic thinned, he pulled out his weapon and took careful aim at the tires of the Audi A4. Two shots. The tires exploded and the car spun out of control, across the meridian, and into oncoming traffic. Perfect.

Tires screeched, metal banged against metal, and he imagined the people in the oncoming tour bus screamed. He chuckled, satisfaction bubbling in his chest. In his rearview mirror, a string of brake lights indicated traffic was coming to a halt. He focused on the small green Kia, now directly in front of him. His niece had no idea her tail was gone. Even if she did, he'd give her no time to react.

Ivar put his foot on the gas, nudged her bumper, and fantasized about fucking her. Perhaps if he gifted Gregor with her infant, it wouldn't be a problem. With the Iesco clan leader dead, she'd be free to mate again. The American hadn't deserved her. Once Ivar had her safely back home in Russia, he'd lock her up. He almost spilled his seed as he rammed the back of the tiny Rio repeatedly with his massive Escalade.

This was going to be fun.

Chapter 19

Zoe relished the quiet as she drove home. Mile after mile of pine trees, interrupted by shore exits and gas stations, soothed her. Soon enough they'd close in on the city and she'd need to put all her focus on driving. Occasionally she glanced at the mirror. Jack kept exactly one car length between them. She could almost make out his discernible frown. He hadn't been happy taking two separate cars, but the solitude was just what she'd needed. Time to think without Jack turning her brain to mush and her body to liquid fire.

A shiver raced down her spine as her thoughts drifted to Jack. She shrugged it off and turned on the air conditioner full blast.

Focus, Zoe. This wasn't just about sex. It was about her whole life being turned upside down. How the hell was she going to integrate witchy-power and a mate into her life?

She couldn't even tell anyone what had happened. Jack and his family had made it very clear that there was a no tolerance policy about blabbing. But really, who would she tell? Her therapist would have her committed, and Nan already thought she had been brainwashed. She was going to freak when she saw the vortex. Shit, what was she going to say when she found out Zoe was pregnant?

Pregnant. It still didn't seem real. She glanced in her rearview mirror and chewed on her lip. Could she really raise a baby with a man she had just met?

No matter how deep her attraction, she didn't know the first thing about him outside of the bedroom. She shook her head and gripped the steering wheel tighter. That wasn't entirely true. He was close to his family and treated them all with kindness and respect. Loyal too, and protective. When he wasn't solstice-crazy, he seemed pretty normal.

Maybe they could make it work.

And maybe pigs could fly.

Relationships equaled love–not sex. And Jack had made it quite clear that love wasn't part of mating.

One thing for certain, she couldn't trust her body to make the decision. Her stepfather had seen to that.

As a kid, before she knew right from wrong, she'd wanted his touch. Asked for it. Zoe shuddered, her stomach cramping at the unbidden thought.

Could she trust Jack? Could she trust herself?

This morning, Jack had been sweet and gentle as he massaged her. But that, too, was all about sex, wasn't it? She wasn't sure. Her sexual perspective was all fucked up. Wasn't that why she was in therapy? For once in her life, she'd like to have a normal relationship without all her baggage showing up on the doorstep like an unwanted guest.

But there was nothing normal about Jack or their relationship. There never could be.

Zoe's head snapped forward, jolting her into the present. A car slammed into hers with a sickening crack of plastic and metal. In the rearview mirror, a dark SUV with black-tinted windows barreled towards her.

What the hell? Where was Jack?

The SUV rammed into her again. Zoe's neck whipped forward and the seat belt cut into her skin. She grabbed the steering wheel, righted her path, and stomped the accelerator to the floor.

Too slow.

On the next hit, her car spun in slow motion. Dirt and grass spewed on her windshield, and then it all stopped. In her vision, the world still rotated. She unbuckled her belt and reached to the passenger seat floor. She unzipped the side pocket of her knapsack and curled her fingers around the mace can.

A vehicle screeched to a halt, and she played dead. She rested her cheek on the hot plastic of the front seat. Leaking gas and burning rubber stung her nostrils and her stomach twisted. She gripped the little canister tighter and made a Herculean effort to stop shaking.

Her driver side door opened "Get out of the car."

She stayed still and waited for him to come closer.

He leaned over, grabbed her arm. The smell of garlic assaulted her nostril, along with the tingling of electric voltage. She turned, opened her eyes, and stared into the nightmare that had scared her shitless for months. How was he still alive?

"Don't move." His smile was triumphant and arrogant. "I used the vortex energy before you were even born. I don't want to injure you or the baby. You come with me. Like a good girl."

Zoe prayed, whipped one hand from behind her back, and maced his face. He screamed and dug his fingers into his eyes.

Immediately, she thrust her feet into his chest and he fell back into the ditch, cursing.

She sprinted for his idling car and snorted a triumphant laugh. She hadn't survived alone in New York without learning a few tricks.

Stones spit from under the tires as she floored the accelerator of the SUV. After a couple of miles, her heart stopped racing and her brain engaged. Where was Jack? The southbound traffic was at a dead standstill.

Oh my God. No, no, no.

She picked up her cell phone, and said, "Call Jack."

A painful eternity of six unanswered rings followed while she held her breath.

"Hi, this is Jack…"

She exhaled. "Jack, Jack. Are you okay?"

"…please leave a message…"

She cursed, hung up, and then spoke into her phone again. "Call Olivia."

"Hi, leave a message for Olivia's Natural Herbal Remedies…"

Damn it all to hell. Didn't anyone pick up their fucking phone anymore? She left a message. "Olivia, nine-one-one. Call me back immediately. Something's happened. Get Josh, too. Get everyone."

Every few seconds, she checked the rearview mirror. How long would it take finger-gun-man to catch up? For a millisecond, she considered calling the police. *Get real.* She was driving a stolen car.

She ached to turn around and find Jack, but the southbound lane was at a dead stop.

Slamming her palms on the steering wheel, she cursed. She'd be a sitting duck if finger-gun-man found her, but she needed to find Jack. Despite the danger, she pulled off at the next rest area, ran into the overcrowded building, and sat down at a table in the far corner of the cafeteria.

Zoe took out her phone and tried Jack again. No answer. Please, please, please be okay.

Two heavyset, blue-haired women sat down at the table next to her. "I heard it was a twelve car pile-up."

Another similarly aged, big-haired matron bobbed her head from another table. "I heard twenty. Two buses across both lanes, one tipped over. Some idiot spun into the south bound lane."

"Probably drunk." The woman clucked her tongue.

"I saw it happen," a man said, smugly. "An Audi spun like a top and then wham." He clapped her hands together and Zoe's gut wrenched. "Two buses hit it, and it scrunched like an accordion. No one could've survived it."

Zoe's body went numb.

The awful truth hit her like a two-by-four. She gasped and barely made it to the bathroom stall before retching.

Her phone rang while she was rinsing her mouth. "Olivia? It's Jack. He's, he's...he's had an accident."

"Whoa, slow down. I got Josh, here, too. On speaker. What're you talking about?"

"I think Jack was hit by a bus, maybe two. I can't find out. The traffic on the parkway is backed up for miles." She leaned against the bathroom wall, shaking, and slowly sunk to the floor.

Josh's voice came out of the little speaker, dry and emotionless. "What is it, Zoe? Do you *think* or do you *know* it was Jack?"

"He was following me, then he wasn't. And I heard a woman describe the Audi that got hit. Josh, he never would've left my tail, unless something really bad had happened." Zoe's throat tightened with the tears she hadn't allowed herself to shed. "The Russian guy...I thought he got blown up with Kyle but he wasn't...he tried to take me, but I maced him and stole his SUV. I'm at a rest stop, a few miles north, but–"

The police band radio squawked in the background, drowning out Josh's voice. He let out a stream of expletives and then commanded, "Get out of there. Get into that car now, Zoe, and drive."

"But Jack needs me." Zoe couldn't catch her breath. Her head was spinning. She wanted someone to come get her and bring her home, not send her away.

Josh spoke slow and direct, as if she was a little kid. "If what you say is true, Jack needs to know you're safe. So do what I say. Do you understand me?"

"Okay."

"Are you south of Point Pleasant?" He sounded very much like a clan leader. Like Jack. And it broke her heart.

"Yes, but–"

"Listen carefully. That man's car probably has GPS, as does your phone. You need to make sure you can't be tracked. When you hang up, turn off your phone and find another ride. Follow the signs for the town of Point Pleasant. Buy a ticket for the city. Leave the car in the station. Do not turn the phone back on and do not go home. Find a place to stay."

"But I have to find Jack..." *This can't be happening.* Pain pierced through her chest in waves. The grief was beyond measure, the not knowing, even worse.

Josh kept talking but Zoe couldn't pay attention. Not now. Not when Jack needed her. "...in command now that Jack is...well, we just don't know. You and your baby are our biggest hope. Don't let Jack down. This is what he would have wanted. Hang up. Do as I say. Now. Pick up a disposable phone and call as soon as you're safe."

The line went dead and she let out a little whimper.

Zoe stood and placed a trembling hand on her stomach. She wasn't just fighting for her own life anymore. She would survive. She had to. For Jack and his unborn child, she would make certain of it.

Chapter 20

Jack's foot itched to go faster. One of the first things he'd do is to buy Zoe a better car.

He hated the fact that she insisted on time away from him, but he'd do whatever it took to make sure she was happy, that she remained his. She was his mate, his love, but it was more than that. He'd never met anyone like her.

She was sexy, intelligent, and funny. Gutsy, too. He doubted any other woman would risk everything for a man she barely knew. It honestly made him nervous. She'd walk directly into any danger without a second thought.

Jack caught a flash of metal in his peripheral vision. A hand with a gun pointed. *Shit.*

He heard two shots and his car veered violently to the left. He tried to twist the steering wheel in the opposite direction, but the car spun out of control. There was a sickening crunch and his head snapped forward. The world rotated in a blur. The car went airborne and the meridian went by in a green flash. A bus horn blasted.

He knew he was going to die. His mind went to Zoe and the baby he would never know. He knew his family would take care of them. At least she'd have a chance at finding happiness with another man.

The vision of some other male raising his child and enjoying Zoe's body yanked him from blissful surrender. That was not going to happen. He called upon the energy that created the universe, scrunched into a small ball, and surrounded himself with an electric shield. Zoe's vortex gave him a level of talent he'd never conjured before.

His car compressed around. Something pierced into his side as his shield started to give. Pain exploded in his head and chest. The sound of metal against metal screamed through his brain. Then silence. Around him, the world faded to black, and he surrendered, his last thoughts of Zoe.

Chapter 21

Zoe sat in finger-gun-man's car and banged her palms on the steering wheel until they stung. How the hell was she supposed to turn off the car's GPS? With a frustrated scream, she let the tears she'd been holding in stream down her face.

She had to find Jack. He couldn't be dead. She wouldn't believe it. She'd go south, even if that meant walking twenty miles.

She grabbed her knapsack, hopped out of the Escalade, and headed back to the building. A tattooed-covered man with a beard reminiscent of an old ZZ Top video strode towards a Harley across her path. She had an epiphany and followed him.

He put on his helmet, and his boots stomped the starter, all the while ignoring her taps on his shoulder. Over the deafening roar of the engine, he leaned back and put the bike in gear. That wouldn't do. She straddled his front tire, reached over the bars, and shoved her hand into his face. The reflection of a sparkling tornado reflected in his visor.

He frowned and shouted over the din, "What the hell do you want?"

"I want a lift to the accident." The exhaust fumes clogged her throat and her eyes stung. She coughed and pointed south.

"Sorry sister. No extra helmet." The biker backed the bike out from between her legs.

Before he could move forward, she threw the vortex, thinking to make a small hole in the parking lot. The ground shook and rumbled like thunder and three cars disappeared into a sinkhole.

The biker's mouth dropped open. "Get on. Shit, what was I drinking last night? What the fuck kind of demon are you?"

"One that wants a ride. Drop me off and I promise to disappear forever." She ran around the back and threw her leg over the back seat.

"Not gonna be an easy ride, sweetheart." The biker gunned the engine and popped a little wheelie. She screeched, almost toppled, but clung to his waist. She tried not to inhale the stench of cigarettes, beer, and sweat.

He raced down the exit ramp on the shoulder's edge. As he darted around traffic, he leaned, and the bike tilted. More than once, she could put her hand to the ground. When he reached the scene of the accident, she stumbled off the bike, and numbly mumbled "thanks." The biker grunted, gunned the engine, and raced away.

A bus lay on its side across two lanes of traffic. A second bus blocked the remaining lane. At least ten ambulances lined up like taxis in front of a tent set up in the meridian. Medics rushed around the chaos. Tow truck operators worked on removing the buses. An elderly couple sat under the shade of meager bushes with empty stares and blank faces. She scanned the scene for Jack's car.

The groan and crack of metal drew her attention.

She nearly retched again when she realized what she was seeing. Jack's car was a misshapen mass of crushed metal, half the size of what it used to be.

"No, no, no!" Her screams tore painfully from her throat.

A young police officer bounded towards her and blocked her from the wreckage.

She clawed at him. "Let me go. You don't understand."

"You know the driver of that car, miss?" His kind but firm hand led her away.

"That was my...my...friend's car. Oh God, is he–" She had to swallow the bile rising in her throat. How could she go on and never feel his arms around her again? Or hear his funny snide remarks? Why had she insisted they take separate cars?

The officer was still talking and she tried to focus on his moving lips. "...miracle, really. We're working with the jaws-of-life but it may take a while. Miss? Did you hear me? He's alive but he floats in and out of consciousness." He moved into her face and stared. "Miss?"

Blood seemed to rush back into her arms and legs. Zoe nodded numbly and let the officer lead her closer to the wreckage.

A large, burly medic looked up when they approached. "Are you Zoe?"

"Yes." Zoe smiled and grimy tears of gratitude ran down her face.

"You can wait over there beside the car. He got rather riled the last time he woke. I think your presence might calm him down while we free him. I'll have someone call you over if he wakes again. In the meantime, report over there." He pointed to a medic truck, and walked towards a woman who held an arm to her chest.

A young man offered her bottled water and indicated where she should sit. She tried to keep up a polite conversation with an elderly couple, but noxious fumes threatened to turn her stomach. She moved away with an apology.

She wanted to text Josh and Olivia, but Josh had said to keep her cell off. She certainly didn't want finger-gun-man to find her again. She was about to ask someone if she could borrow their phone, when the officer nearest Jack's car beckoned her over with a shout and a wave.

She prepared for the worst as she slowly approached the gnarled mess. Jack's moans made her run to the gaping hole. An alien cocoon blanketed him in metal. Oddly, there was no blood and his cuts seemed minor.

"I'm here." Her legs almost gave out with the rush of relief.

"Zoe?" Jack's voice was muffled, his head faced down, his body in a fetal position.

She put her hand through the sharp mass of metal and rubbed the rough stubble of his cheek. "It's me."

Jack sighed with a whoosh of air. "You're okay."

She smiled through the tears stinging her eyes.

"They're going to get you out of there. You're going to be fine."

"I'm so fucking tired," he said brokenly. "Lost too much energy. Understand? My body needs to recoup..." His voice was a weak whisper. "Need Olivia."

Zoe got it. Leaving her hand on his cheek, she closed her eyes and pulsed healing energy into him until she had no more to give. She braced herself against the car and held his head until he fell asleep.

A medic put an arm under her shoulder and helped her away. "He's going to be okay, Miss. But we'll know better once we get him out of there."

"Can I stay with him?" She turned to the annoying beep-beep-beep of a huge tow truck backing up.

"This could still take a couple hours. You're going to have to step back onto the green." The medic led her back onto the meridian. The multiple flashing emergency lights caught in her peripheral vision, causing an odd sense of vertigo. The smell of oil, gasoline and burnt rubber added to her discomfort.

Zoe placed her head between her legs and sat on the green that stretched for miles. The pneumatic motor of the jaws-of-life growled and the car frame screamed and screeched in protest. Cars slowed on the north side of the parkway as they passed the scene to rubberneck. Occasionally, brakes squealed and horns honked.

Josh's voice boomed above her. "What the hell are you doing here?"

She squinted into the now midday sun. Olivia was there, too, wearing a disapproving frown.

"He's my mate. I needed to be here." Zoe jutted out her jaw.

"We snuck right up on you. Do you have a death wish?" Josh scolded.

"She's safe. That's all that matters." Olivia sat down beside her and placed an arm over her shoulder.

Together they waited while Jack's car was split apart. Eventually he was extracted from the wreckage into a waiting ambulance, and Zoe felt like she could breathe again.

Chapter 22

Jack woke to Zoe's gentle snoring. Her body snuggled into his chest, and the scent of fresh strawberries mixed with an overpowering antiseptic smell. He opened his heavy eyes to an unknown bed and an unknown room. An IV line strung from a hole in his arm to a plastic bag above. Metal bars framed the sides of the bed. Outside the room, a nurse sat at a desk.

He wiggled each of his appendages and one didn't respond. *Shit.* He extracted a tingling arm from under Zoe and flexed his hand. *Not broken. Just asleep.*

Zoe stirred, yawned, and flashed him a sleepy grin. "You're awake."

"How long have I been out?" He touched her mussed hair and looked into her sunken, exhausted eyes.

"Not too long." She was lying.

"It's dark out. Last thing I remember it was morning and I was driving home–" His chest clenched as memories assailed him. "An accident."

"I thought I'd lost you." Her voice was clogged with emotion.

She looked away but he pulled her chin back towards him. Her big brown eyes glistened like obsidian in the dark. She leaned up, parted her lips, and he tasted heaven. She squirmed closer on the tiny bed and squeezed him until his bruised ribs complained.

He didn't care. He wanted her right where she was. Forever. "Was anyone hurt?"

"Mostly minor injuries, but a couple were hurt pretty seriously when a tour bus flipped on its side." She sat up and rested her soft hand on the side of his face. "They say you lost a tire and spun out. Do you remember anything?"

Jack closed his eyes, his head pounded, and he tried to remember. "I crossed the meridian and put my shields on max. That little vortex saved my ass. Other than that, everything is foggy."

"I remember being worried about you." He moved his IV tube so he could pull her back down to his chest. "I need to take you home, angel. Something's not right. Please get me out of here."

"Your family's sleeping in the lobby. I have to go tell them you're okay." She maneuvered herself off the bed, and frowned down at him. "I'm so sorry. This is all my fault. If I had shared your ride, like you wanted, none of this would've happened."

"You don't know that." Jack grabbed a hand to tug her back.

"Yeah I do. It's me he wants. You, he just wants out of the way."

"Who, Zoe? Who was it? What the hell happened?" Jack sat up, suddenly very awake.

"The stalker guy." She met his gaze with eyes wide. "He didn't die in the explosion. After he ran you off the road, he did the same to me."

Jack caught his breath and swore.

"He wants me alive. I think he wants our baby." She took a step away, her eyes haunted.

Shit. Jack rubbed her cold fingers and brooded over how best to kill the bastard.

"I've been thinking. He must've known all along I was a witch. Even before *I* knew. The first time I saw him was right before my parent's funeral. How could that be?"

"Not sure, honey, but we're going to find out. Don't worry. Go get Josh."

"Okay."

"Zoe." Jack closed his eyes as he remembered her healing touch in the wrecked car and the overwhelming relief he felt when he knew she was safe. He knew his words were going to be inadequate even as they left his mouth. "Thanks for coming back to check on me."

"I had to." Zoe's brows furrowed. "I love you."

She turned quickly and dashed out of the room.

Jack stared at the void and wondered what he might've said if she'd stayed. Relieved that he didn't have to face that issue in that moment, he picked up the phone beside his bed and dialed.

A gruff voice answered on the second ring. "Detective O'Brien here."

"Hey Liam. It's Jack Fialko."

"What's going on? I thought you were taking some vacation time?"

"I was. Some ass-wipe of a stalker has been after my… girlfriend. Tried to run me off the parkway yesterday to get to her. Probably saw it on the news?"

"Shit. You okay?"

"Yeah. I'm heading back to New York and could use that new super-computer you guys installed when we get there. I'll have Josh send you everything I know."

"Sure. Give me a shout when you get to town."

"One more thing?"

"Yeah?"

"Josh is going to be arranging more security. Can you let NYPD know the situation?"

"That can be arranged. Anything else?"

"Yeah. Pray we get this guy before it's too late."

Chapter 23

High up in the Hummer Josh rented, Jack drove while Zoe studied the road's reflection in the passenger side mirror. In her mind, the dark SUV barreled towards them, intent on death. In the real world, Jase followed three car lengths behind.

Zoe shuddered. "You should've stayed in the hospital for another day."

Jack chuckled. Today his light brown eyes flashed with golden flecks, reflecting the sun, and the stripes in his silk tie. His dark pants held a sharp center crease and an expensive navy blazer hung under plastic in the back. She missed beach-bum-Jack, but go-to-work-Jack would've had her creaming, if it weren't for the sense of danger she couldn't shake.

He smiled her way as if reading her mind.

"How do you know we're safe? That stalker could be anywhere." Zoe wished she was home already. Her stomach was tied in knots.

Jack patted the steering wheel, and smirked. "He's no match for the two of us and this big baby."

Zoe glanced over her shoulder at the raven-haired teenager in the backseat. The girl gave her a tentative smile, then looked back out the window. Jase had found her wandering the parking lot after the explosion. Apparently, she was the girl Kyle had convinced Jack he'd mated with. Zoe shuddered, she couldn't have been more than thirteen. Zoe had tried to have a conversation with her, but the girl's English was limited to two-word sentences. All Zoe really knew about her was that her name was Erina.

"Why are you bringing the girl back to New York? I thought she was staying with your parents."

Jack frowned and his eyes flickered to the rearview mirror. "Josh thinks she might have something to do with the Russian. We'll keep her safe, find out what she knows, where she came from, then send her back home."

The girl tapped Zoe on the shoulder. With eyes wide, she shook her head back and forth and mouthed the word, *no*.

Zoe nodded, made a calming motion with both palms down, and said to Jack, "She understands us, you know. Did you find out anything more?"

"She was supposed to end up at a Pennsylvania bible camp but our stalker friend apparently arranged a detour." Jack maneuvered their mammoth vehicle easily in and out of the fast lane.

"And?"

Jack's expression turned grim and he swiped a hand across his face. "She and several other girls were no doubt packing heroine in their stomachs on the trip over from Europe."

"No way. That is so not right." Zoe clenched her fists.

"From what I can gather, she was sold for that and prostitution." He said it so off-the-cuff. Like he was talking about the weather.

Flashbacks of another childhood caught her by surprise. Zoe closed her eyes and leaned back, breathing hard.

Jack took her hand and squeezed gently. "Are you going to be sick? Should I pull over?"

"If you send her home, won't they just sell her again?" Zoe did her best to sit up, open her eyes, and dispel the awful memories.

Jack shrugged. "Nothing we can do about it. She belongs to her family. Her government will be notified. I have charities overseas that–"

"No." Zoe shook her head and looked back at the girl, whose mouth was drawn down in a deep frown.

"No, what?" Jack peered at her.

"No, you're not sending her back."

"Not my call, honey. I don't have the authority to keep her in the country." Jack used that placating and condescending voice that she hated.

She glared him down but his eyes were on the road. "Well I think that's total bullshit."

"Just because I have some talent with energy, doesn't mean I can manipulate the whole government to my will. I can't fix every bad thing in the whole wide world."

"We're not sending that little girl back into a life of prostitution. End of story."

"I never said that. I said she needs to be with her family." Jack gripped the steering wheel tightly. His neck muscles twitched just below his ears.

How could she make him understand? This was about more than just the girl. It was about her. If only there had been someone there to save her, to protect her.

Could she trust him enough to tell him what had happened? She shivered and looked out the window.

"Do mated men ever stray?" She picked at a loose string on the seam of her jeans.

He turned sharply to look at her with a deep frown.

"I guess they could, but why? The sex would never be better than with their mate." Jack smirked a little too arrogantly.

"What if a couple isn't compatible outside of the bedroom?"

"They figure it out. A mate is more than a husband or a wife, more than just being a lover. I keep trying to tell you that." He rubbed her leg and gave her a dimpled smile. "There's other reasons for holding onto the relationship. We're a small group. Through the centuries, our race has been hunted and tortured. We have to mate sensibly. When there's a powerful line, like ours, it's our duty to see it passed on and ensure the next generation's safety."

How well he spliced love right out of the equation. "So even if you find you don't *like* me, you won't leave?"

Jack answered sharply, "Is that what this is all about? You're afraid I won't stay with you?"

Damn the man was thick.

No. I'm afraid you won't ever love me.

"I still have trust issues." She didn't mean for that to slip out.

"Issues?" He honed in on *that* topic like a heat-seeking missile. *Figures.*

"Yeah. Big time trust issues," she mumbled.

"You don't trust me?"

Dammit Jack, it's not always all about you.

She shrugged and looked away.

Jack's response sounded more like a growl than a man's voice. Stormy-eyed, he pulled the Hummer off the parkway at the next exit, and parked next to a gas station-convenience store. Jase stayed right behind them. Jack got out of the vehicle and approached Jase's car. They spoke for a moment, then Jack motioned for Zoe to get out.

Zoe slunk further into the front seat and stared at the roof. *Okay, you pissed him off. Mission accomplished. Now what?*

He crossed his arms across his chest and waited. When she didn't move, he opened the passenger door.

"Get out so I can talk to you. You're impossible today. I don't feel comfortable stopping here but I can't drive when you're like this."

"You know, Jack, you can be pretty unreasonable too. Every time I try to explain stuff to you, you get mad." Her throat tightened and she squeezed her eyes shut, willing the tears back into her head.

"Crying won't solve anything. Get out and talk to me." Jack reached up, cupped her butt, and tugged her forward. He lifted her by the waist and their bodies rubbed intimately as she dropped to the ground. "Tell me what's going on in that head of yours."

Zoe wished she had nothing to confess except her blossoming love. Why had she brought this up to begin with? Erina peeked her head over the seat, and Zoe remembered.

"You won't want to stay with me if I tell you." She looked down and fidgeted with a button on his shirt.

Jack pulled up on her chin. "Tell me what's bothering you. Whatever it is, at least give me the chance to try and fix it."

Fix it? She shook her head. There was no fixing the brokenness inside her. "I c-can't. You'll despise me."

"Never." He cupped her cheeks with his palms and shook his head vehemently.

She needed to just spit it out. Get it out of the way, so it wouldn't hang between them. She took a deep breath.

"I was abused as a kid." She bit her lip hard and tasted blood. Her throat constricted. She looked over to the vehicle where Erina watched them with wide, uncertain eyes. "I was a bit younger than the girl when it started. My father–" She winced. "Now I know he was my adoptive father, but it doesn't make it any less wrong."

"He hit you?"

"No."

Zoe knew when he understood because his face turned white and his breath came out in a hiss.

"Fuck." Jack scrubbed his fingers through his hair and blew out a long breath. "Did he... did he rape you?"

"No, but, in a way, it was worse. He touched me. Always and often. It went on for years. As long as I can remember until I finally left home." She hunted his expression and only saw eyes that were filled with silent compassion. That gave her courage to continue. "I've never told anybody how young I was. Not even my therapist. I was nine or ten, maybe less. I honestly don't remember. I was too little to even understand the nature of that kind of touching. He told me it was normal and that he loved me."

"Didn't your mother know?"

"She walked in on it more than once, but pretended she saw nothing." Zoe frowned, pursed her lips together and squeezed her eyes shut. Memories sucked.

"Did you ever try to tell someone?"

Zoe studied the ant hole at her feet. She sympathized with how they worked like hell to fix damage that could never be undone.

"I tried to confront my mother in my teens and get her to help me. She refused. So when I was old enough I left. I've been on my own ever since."

Jase tapped the roof and lifted his eyebrows.

"I'm sorry angel, but we need to get back on the road." Jack hugged her tight and then motioned for her to get back in the car.

When they were on the road for a while, he asked into the lengthening silence, "Did you try the authorities?"

"Why? My mother was under his power, too. She'd lie to protect him. It would be my word against his *and* hers. I had no proof."

"How did you survive?"

"I'd been stealing a little from his bank account for years and had his bank card. I cleaned him out, went to New York, and started working at the only thing I knew how to do. Breaking and entering networks." She paused and grinned. "Craigslist is full of opportunities for an enterprising sort. That's where I met Nan. We were breaking into the same network."

Jack didn't smile back. He just drove with his jaw ticking.

Zoe gave him time to digest everything.

"I don't know how, but I'm going to spend my life making it right for you."

Her mouth dropped open. "You still want to stay with me after everything I told you?"

"You did nothing wrong." Jack flicked his eyes off the road and they gleamed with fierceness. His lips went thin. "My only regret is the bastard isn't alive, so I could cut his dick off and make him eat it."

Zoe's lips twitched. That was probably one of the nicest things he'd ever said to her. She peeked over her shoulder at Erina who watched them with dark, uncertain eyes.

"Now you understand why I can't let you send her back?" Zoe said.

Jack's hand rested on her thigh.

"Don't worry." He glanced into the rearview at the girl. "I won't send her back, unless she wants to go."

Erina grinned broadly and Zoe couldn't help but smile back.

Chapter 24

Jack yawned, turned down the tunnel, and stopped at the yellow line. Fluorescents lit the dingy underground parking and a four-foot graying poster listed the outrageous hourly prices. His brother, Jase, parked behind him a minute later.

The elderly garage attendant, Sam, gave a big toothless grin and shuffled over. "Welcome home, Mr. Fialko. Will you need help with your bags?"

"Yes, and call my driver. I'll be back down in fifteen minutes." Jack stretched the cramp in his leg.

"Sure." Sam nodded. "Detective O'Brien is waiting in the lobby."

"Thank you." Jack handed Sam his keys with a twenty.

In the backseat, Erina bounced up and down, waiting for him to release the child locks. She hopped down in a flash and ran to Jase who gave her a stick of gum.

Jack opened Zoe's door. She smiled seductively and waited for him to help her down. He obliged and let her body slowly slide the length of his. He gave her waist a tight squeeze.

"That's me. Number Eight-Fifty." He pointed to his co-op.

Jase came up behind them, his phone in his hand. "The lawyers are all pitching a hissy-fit about moving our money into the Caymans. I hope you know what you're doing."

"Someone more powerful than me is out there. Clan law hasn't changed. If I die, winner takes all."

"That kind of shit won't hold up in court," Jase said tightly.

"If you don't abide, all the clans will rise up. We'd do the same. We've talked about this for years."

"I never thought it would happen." Jase frowned and his eyebrows furrowed. "Fuck, you're my brother. I don't want to lose you."

A doorman held the door open. Zoe's eyes went wide and her mouth dropped open. Jack couldn't help but smile. He couldn't wait to spoil her rotten. Give her everything she'd ever desired.

"I don't want to lose me either. I'm just taking precautions. Most everything you can buy back legally when I'm gone. It's the charity money I worry most about." Jack slapped his younger brother on the back. "C'mon. There's O'Brien."

Detective O'Brien sat in one of six overstuffed chairs in the lobby. He rose with the grace of a cat. "There's my favorite student."

Jack braced for the solid pat on the back that would've sent most men sliding to the wall. When it came, he laughed. He gave an almost equal one back.

"It's great to see you, Liam. Meet my mate, Zoe, and you know my brother, Jase." Jack gave a small nod to the girl. "And this is Erina."

Despite O'Brien's dark, good looks and sensual demeanor, he held himself with a sense of detachment. But when his gaze landed on the girl, his blue eyes softened, and he gave her a genuine smile.

After signing them in at the desk, Jack walked them to the elevator, and pressed eight. He said to Zoe, "Liam is my martial arts instructor. Has been for years. He's also JTTF."

"JTTF?"

"Joint terrorism task force. New York's finest working harmoniously with the FBI." O'Brien winked.

"Hey, you wouldn't by any chance know Nanobyte? She just got hired by the FBI in New York."

"Who doesn't? She worked my last case with me. I swear the woman's brain is half-computer."

"She's my best friend." Zoe's face lit up.

"Can't wait to compare notes." O'Brien's light blue eyes watched her with amused fascination.

Jack felt a twinge in his chest. He put a possessive arm around his mate and O'Brien laughed at the obvious move. Good thing the elevator door opened so Jack wouldn't have to eat the words he almost uttered. He unlocked the door that led into the foyer and let everyone in.

"You live here?" Zoe held Erina's hand and put her nose to his latest acquisition, an Arizona landscape of the rising sun over desert cactus, and gave an appreciative smile.

His insides melted. She liked his favorite painting. That bode well for the rest of his apartment. He led them into the living room.

"Go ahead and sit. I'll ask Joan to make us a quick snack before we head out."

"You have a cook?" Her eyes widened, then her mouth curved down in a frown. "How many servants do you have?"

"Employees, not servants." His brother laughed. "And he's got a pilot, a personal assistant, and if you count all the companies he owns, including this building, he probably has–"

"It doesn't matter," Jack said, seeing the uncertainty in her eyes as she took it all in.

Zoe groaned and mumbled something under her breath. Jack said nothing. She was here with him and that's all that mattered.

* * *

Zoe had never seen anything like Jack's apartment, except maybe in the movies. Her whole flat would fit into the foyer alone. How the hell was she going to fit into a life like this? Jack held out his hand and escorted her into the kitchen.

One wall held floor to ceiling windows and a balcony. From the eighteenth floor, she could see the entrance to Central Park.

Jack was saying something about the Wi-Fi password but it was too hard to focus. She couldn't shut out how friggin' loaded the guy was. It was one thing to read about it online, and quite another to walk into your new mate's home worth millions.

"Are you okay" Jack watched her, his head tilted slightly, a frown on his handsome face.

"Sorry. I'm a bit overwhelmed."

He pulled her to his chest and whispered into her ear, "Angel, it'll be alright. We're together in this."

"Okay." Zoe nodded, but she couldn't shake the anxiety.

"We're heading out now," Jack said, releasing her, then scooped a cookie from the plate on the island and handed it to Erina. The girl's face lit up. "O'Brien found a safe house for the girl. I'm going to get her settled, and take care of a few things. Joan will be here if you need anything."

Zoe glanced at the middle-aged woman who stood beside the stove stirring the contents of a large pot. She wondered if the woman knew about Jack's family and what he was—what she was.

Jack slid his fingers along her chin and brushed his lips softly against hers. Little zings of electricity pulsed through her, and he gave her the half-dimpled smile that sent shivers down the length of her body.

"I'll be back soon." His voice held the promise of what his gaze suggested, and her knees went a little weak.

Would she ever get use to the power he had over her body?

After they left, she sat down at the kitchen table. She linked to the internet and tried to get lost in her work. Usually the constant world of variables and conditionals gave her comfort. But she couldn't stop her mind from wandering. Jack in the ocean. Jack kissing her. Jack in her bed, touching her. *Argh!*

Joan didn't seem to notice her discomfort. She went about her business, cutting onions, veggies, and sausage, then left them to simmer on the stove. She puttered about the apartment, humming.

Around noon, the older woman placed a Cobb salad on the table beside her laptop. "You need to eat."

"How long have you worked for Jack?" Zoe pushed her work aside, muttered a thank you, and picked up the fork. She would never get use to someone serving her.

"I use to change his diapers." Joan's eyes went misty and soft. "My family has taken care of his clan for generations. He's good man."

Zoe nodded and looked down at her salad. "What was he like as a child?"

"Much like he is today. Handsome. Stubborn. Arrogant. Caring. Always looking out for the less fortunate."

"I read online that he gives away millions."

"Oh, that's just the tip of the iceberg. He facilitates with governments. Uses his influence to make sure his money goes where it's intended. He visits all those places, too. Here let me show you."

Joan reached for Zoe's laptop and brought up a webpage with Jack's face all over it.

They hadn't been apart for so long since the mating. She couldn't believe how much she missed him. She perused page after page full of pictures. Jack in China looking for earthquake survivors, Jack in Haiti, Jack with a smiling child after 'spina bifida' surgery. *When did he find time for all that?*

"If he had his way, this website wouldn't exist." Joan peered up over her reading glasses sounding as proud as any mother. "His publicists insist so they can continue to increase awareness for their causes."

"I don't think I know him at all." She gave a weary breath. "He never said anything about what he does for a living. When you're down at the shore, it's like the real world doesn't even exist. But here…"

"Love can blossom in unexpected places." Joan gave her a sympathetic smile and patted Zoe's hand.

"Maybe," Zoe murmured, but even as she said it, she wasn't convinced.

Love wasn't something Jack was willing to give.

Chapter 25

Jack smiled when he found Zoe in the kitchen, bent over her laptop, typing in a focused frenzy.

"I missed you." He leaned over and inhaled her essence. She let out a soft sigh. When he nibbled the top of her ear, she turned and all but devoured his lips. She stood, and melted into his embrace. "How's my mate?"

"I'm better now." Her eyes flickered with a surge of desire, then clouded over. "How's Erina?"

"She's safe."

Zoe cocked her head and pursed her lips into a little frown.

"I made a promise. Nothing will happen to her." He kissed her nose and pulled away. "I've put a team together to research how we can best help girls like her." He walked to the stove and uncovered the blue ceramic saucepan. "I'm starving."

"You're setting up a new charity?" Her voice broke with emotion and her eyes grew misty.

"You said it's important to you."

For a moment, he glimpsed the pain and nightmares that she had held inside herself for far too long. He forgot about his rumbling stomach and pulled her towards him, and enveloped her in his embrace. He brushed his lips against hers and infused her with a gentle blast of heat. He dug in for a deeper kiss and his tongue met hers playfully.

He couldn't believe how she affected him.

"Are you hungry?" he asked, when her stomach rumbled.

"For you? Yes," she said, nipping at his bottom lip. With a wince she looked at the pot on the stove. "I'm allergic to tomatoes, but I didn't want to hurt Joan's feelings."

"What else are you allergic to?" Jack cursed himself for not asking sooner.

"I love strawberries, tomatoes and chocolate but they make my face break out into icky acne. Something about histamines. And some red wines give me a migraine." She let out a soft moan as he kissed his way down her neck. "Red food dye can, too, and anything with sodium nitrate."

She conversed as if she had no idea how hard he was for her. His erection pressed solidly into her abs and she pretended not to notice. So that was her game tonight. He played along, ignoring the fact her eyes dilated and her cheeks flushed.

"That's quite a list. How did you figure all that out?" His hands helped themselves to the soft skin at her waist and he teased her with an index finger just under her bra band.

She closed her eyes for a second, whimpered, and then kept talking as if they were in the middle of a crowded mall. He had to give her credit. She was good.

"I just kept a diary. I really hate migraines." She made a little mewling sound when his thumb brushed over her taut nipple. "How about you? Any allergies?"

"Just shellfish." Jack smirked and blew warm breath into her ear.

She moaned, put her hand to just above where he ached for her, and sent her energy into him.

Oh God.

She smirked. "Any shellfish?"

Another blast of energy left his balls tightening painfully, and his cock straining against the fabric of his slacks.

"Shellfish...Blow up like a balloon." He clenched his teeth. She was winning this game hands down. His hands found his favorite curves. Her hip bone, the round curves of her breast.

"Okay, no shellfish."

"What else don't you like?" He alluded to something quite different than food with his tone.

"That's a pretty long list." She snuggled closer but he knew it was because her legs were giving out. Her hands were in his hair and he could feel her trembling against him.

"I want to know." He cupped his hand between her legs, felt the heated warmth through the denim. "What don't you like?"

"Peas. Brussel sprouts. Rhubarb–" She tiled her head back, closed her eyes and sucked in a sharp breath when he infused her with another blast, this time between her legs. She rocked against him. "Mmmm. And arrogant men."

He chuckled against her lips. "None?"

"Maybe one." She nipped at his bottom lip, then wrapped her arms around his shoulders, and deepened the kiss.

She made him so damn hard that he physically ached for her. His cock throbbed in demand and his muscles tensed. He gripped the material of her shirt and pulled it over her head.

"What about Joan?" Zoe whimpered.

"Gone home." He ran a hand over her breast and squeezed gently.

"Good." She cupped him in her hand through his pants and sent an electric pulse of energy through his groin.

His hips jerked and his entire body quivered for her. He growled low in his throat, pulled back from her kiss and buried his mouth against her neck. "I can't get enough of you."

He needed her in a way that terrified him.

Clenching his teeth, he removed the last of their clothes. He raked his gaze of the soft lines of her body. Fuck, she was stunning. Standing in his kitchen naked, hunger in her eyes, he swore he'd never seen anything more perfect in his entire life.

He knelt before her, and ran his tongue along the soft skin, kissing a trail down her stomach, hips, inner thighs. She moaned when he parted the warm folds with his tongue, sliding against the entrance.

"Intoxicating," he whispered, against her damp heat. "So fucking beautiful."

"Jack," she cried out hoarsely, arching against his mouth. Her fingers threaded through his hair. She gasped when he slid a finger inside of her. Her body shivered and jerked in response to his touch. She gripped the edge of the counter, and he felt her legs tremble.

"What do you need?"

"More," she panted. "I need more of you."

In a swift movement, he scooped her up and carried her to his bedroom. He placed her on the bed, and she arched for him, whimpering in need, her eyes closed. Her legs parted and she gripped the base of his cock.

He held himself above her until she opened her eyes and met his gaze.

"You're mine." He brushed his lips over hers. "Say it."

"Yours," she whimpered.

Heat wrapped around him and he let out a moan of pleasure as he sunk into her. Pleasure sliced through his senses. God, she felt good. There was nothing better than the feeling of being inside her.

His tongue rolled against her nipple and her head arched back. He thrust deeper, harder, until she cried out his name. Her legs tightened against his hips. She gazed up at him, face flushed, eyes dark with hunger.

With deep, furious strokes, he buried his cock inside her. He found himself spiraling completely out of control. He felt her orgasm rising, and thanked the Goddess above. He wouldn't last much longer.

Her flesh convulsed and rippled around his cock. She clamped around him and cried out. Ecstasy rocked him to the core, tightening his muscles and stealing his sanity. He let out a harsh cry as he thrust one last time, then erupted in heavy spurts of mind-blowing pleasure.

There wasn't an ounce of energy left in his body when he collapsed beside her. She snuggled against his chest, and he wrapped his arms around her shoulders, drawing her closer.

His eyes closed and he started to drift off. He could hear Zoe's steady breath. Feel the beat of her heart against his chest.

"I love you." The words were a whisper, so soft he almost didn't hear them.

Jack cringed inwardly at the words he knew she desperately wanted him to return.

But what was love, other than a fleeting emotion that could destroy a man's sanity? He'd given into it once. Never again.

Why complicate what he had with his mate?

Zoe wanted to be loved. He didn't fault her for it. But what she didn't understand was that his oath, their bond, was worth more than three silly little words. Jack would protect her, and their child, so long as there was breath in his body.

Chapter 26

Jack was surprised that Zoe stayed put all week. Maybe he'd throw some more work to that little internet company she worked for. She seemed to be happiest when she was busy. Lying on his king size bed, with her wrapped in his legs, he didn't think he'd ever felt happier.

"I going to hit the gym." She glanced at the time on the phone, then tried to get untangled from the sheets and his legs.

"There's one in the building. Third floor."

"It doesn't have what I need." Naked, she stood and stretched.

Jack would have her back underneath him if she stretched like that again. He cleared his throat. "What kind of machine do you want? I'll have it delivered tomorrow. This afternoon if you like."

Her eyes danced when her gaze drifted south to his arousal. "No machine. Zumba class. I'll grab a cab."

"I can't let you out of the house."

"Not negotiable."

"You think that creep gave up following you?" Jack jumped out of bed and stood directly in front of her with his arms crossed.

She walked around him and into the bathroom. "I'm not changing my life to that extent. I'm going to Zumba."

She exited a few minutes later. Her hair was up in a ponytail and she was wearing a pair of skimpy shorts and workout bra.

Blood rushed south. "What about the baby, Zoe? You're going to play roulette with its life too?"

She met his annoyed gaze. "If you're worried about our safety then come with me."

He let go, pulled on a pair of boxers, followed her into the kitchen, and grumbled, "I'm not doing fucking Zumba."

She shrugged, tossed her head, and found her sneakers.

"Okay, fine." Jack sighed. He was just getting her to accept him into her life. Going to her gym was a small concession. He picked up the phone to call his driver and alert security.

Less than an hour later, Jack watched through the large plate glass window that separated the classroom from the rest of the gym. Zoe gyrated and humped to the music with the others. He was shocked. There were ladies older than his mother shaking their boobs and jamming their hips into the air.

"Holy fuck."

Another man using the machine next to his heard his oath. They both faced the glassed-in classroom. "You said it. I wouldn't mind bein' under any of those ladies if they would shake it like that over me."

Jack's first inclination was to hit the man with a burst of energy that would double him over with a stomachache for life, but the man wasn't being overly lecherous. He was only speaking what every man in the gym was thinking. The dance should be fucking illegal.

With an irritated sigh, Jack took a machine within viewing distance and tried not to ogle. Dammit, though, he was only ogling his own mate. He watched her sexy dancing emulate what she could do in bed and worked his way over to the weights. There was too much going on in his gym shorts to stay on the treadmill.

Finally, the music slowed to a sexy Latin beat. Even though the class was full, and the lights low, she was easy to locate. Tall, lots of leg, and long dark hair. Minutes later she exited the room, laughing with her classmates, all sweaty and high on endorphins. She waved goodbye and spotted him by the weights.

She sauntered over to him covered with a sheen of sweat and smelling of strawberry musk. Her face positively glowed and her eyes sparkled.

Jack placed the barbell in the rack and put his arm possessively around her shoulder. "You know every male eye in the gym from fifteen to eighty is on you right now?"

She hit him gently on the shoulder. "You're not jealous are you?"

He shrugged and tightened his hold. "Do you do that dance thing often?"

"Whenever I can. Why?"

Jack shook his head in response and walked her towards the juice bar. "Want something to drink?"

"It's way too expensive in here."

"Humor me." Jack bought her a three dollar bottle of water and then continued to lead her into the seating area where a huge plate glass window overlooked the expansive gym. He stood with her in full view of the glass and gave her a full body heated kiss.

"What was that for?" She smiled and caught her breath.

"Staking my claim with the sexiest woman in that heathen dance class."

"Heathen?" She smirked.

"It looked like you were practicing humping." Jack scowled at her.

"Heathen humping?" She broke into laughter. The sound pealed through the refreshment area with a high pitched ring. It was the first time he had heard her just let go and be joyous with no inhibitions. It was so infectious he couldn't help but join her. Even the young man at the juice bar smiled.

"You should do that more often." Jack gazed into her deep brown eyes. He never noticed before how the light caught in them with flecks of gold.

"Heathen hump?" She grinned mischievously.

"No. Laugh like that. It's amazing." He moved a silky strand of hair away from her ear, then leaned and whispered, "You've tortured me long enough. I want some of what you were doing in that room. I want to feel that over me. Now."

He grabbed her upper arm and led her quickly towards the change rooms, opened the door marked 'families only' and then pushed her into the room. He turned and locked the door. "Show me." He pushed her against the wall, right next to the changing table, and put his hands on either side of her head.

"Show me how you can move like that on me."

She giggled. "In here?"

Jack slipped his hands under her stretchy workout bra. Her breasts easily slipped into his grasp and he caressed them, pinching the nipples. Damn he loved the way they hardened for him.

The moan that escaped her lips was filled with desperation. She raised her arms for him and pulled her wet top off. Her nails dug into his back, and she wrapped one leg around his calf, locking him tightly against her body. Jack cupped his hand to her ass, enjoying how she tied herself around him.

"I want you, Zoe. Don't make me wait." He released her leg, and slid her shorts off.

"Don't wait," she whimpered, tangling her fingers in his hair.

He conjured heat, a fireball of lust, and rubbed it into his fingers. He waited until she opened her eyes, then cupped his palm over the warm folds between her legs. When she arched and moaned, he released the energy–the full heat of his desire. She arched against him and let out a sharp cry.

Her legs opened wider and she wrapped them tightly around his waist until he gasped at her strength. At some point, his shorts had fallen to the floor, and lay around his ankles. His cock nudged greedily at her entrance.

With a playful smile, she produced a small vortex, and gave a triumphant laugh as it wrapped around his erection, then shot through his body. Lust tore up his spine and his muscles clenched. He sucked in his breath and nearly came. His cock was so damn hard it ached. A bead of cum escaped over the tip. That was all the play he could endure. He buried himself inside her, and she sank onto him with a frantic moan.

She bucked against him, hard, fast. He covered her mouth with a kiss when she cried out his name.

Suddenly, thousands of little muscles convulsed around him, sucking and pulling. Jack heard himself moan and he plunged into the abyss of nirvana, exploding his seed into her. The world receded for him and the lights in the room went out. A small neon-purple vortex hung in the air, then snapped to pop out of existence.

"Holy shit." She rested her head against his chest. Her flesh pulsed around his cock and it throbbed back.

He was never going to let her go. She could screw him into oblivion and he would die a happy man.

Eventually, he untwisted her legs from around his waist and kissed her nose.

"We should go before someone needs this room. I'll get the car. Do me a favor and wait right here until I ping you." He put a new iPhone in her hand.

Zoe sighed, peeled herself off the shelf, and reached down to find her pants. "You think that guy is still close?"

"Until I know for sure, we're not taking any chances."

Chapter 27

Jack lay awake, not quite ready for sleep. Holding Zoe close, he listened to her soft breaths. She kicked his leg in her sleep and rolled away from him. Needing to feel her touch, he turned on his side and pulled her backside against his chest. She moaned and let out a blood-curdling shout.

"Don't touch me," she hissed viciously, hitting and scratching at him.

Her voice didn't even sound like her. *What the hell?*

"Zoe, wake up."

A small fireball shot out from her right hand and blasted his dresser, which burst into flames.

Jack jumped out of bed, threw a blanket over the small blaze, and ran to the kitchen for the fire extinguisher.

When he moved back towards the bed, she was weeping into her pillow. The bed rocked with her movements.

"Hey, it was just a dream." He tried to touch her gently but she slapped his hand away.

"Touch me again and I'll scream."

Jack swallowed hard. She was dreaming. Caught in the nightmare of the past. He was afraid to move, to make a sound, in case she zapped into her powers again.

"Get away. Please." Zoe collapsed on the bed and sobbed inconsolably.

He watched her return to a more restful sleep and remembered with guilt how he had manipulated her into mating with him. If he'd known she'd been abused as a child, he would've gone at things a lot differently.

She'd mentioned wanting a therapist and now understood how important it might be. His blackened dresser stood out as a scary reminder. She might burn the whole building down around them, along with their baby. She could go to bed and never wake up. A lump formed in his throat and he swallowed hard. She was right when she said she was a walking, talking napalm bomb.

Zoe stirred on the bed and focused her sleepy eyes on him. "What's wrong?"

Jack sat down on the edge of the bed and pushed the sweat soaked hair off her face.

"You're scaring me," she said, sitting up. Her eyes went huge when she noticed the torched dresser. "Oh my God, did I do that?"

"You had a nightmare."

"A nightmare?" Her face was pale and her bottom lip began to tremble. She looked down at her hands, to the dresser, then back at Jack. "I could have killed us."

He wrapped her in his arms and pulled her onto his lap. She lay limp against him, but he could feel the panic rising within her. He was aware of the memories and fears that haunted her. He just hadn't realized how deep the wounds were.

If he could give her time to heal, he would. But they didn't have time. Not when her powers were so volatile.

"I'll make an appointment tomorrow with a therapist."

She tensed in his arms. "I already have one."

"Not one that you can talk to about what you are."

"But—"

He pressed his lips against hers to stop her protest, then pulled back with a small shake of his head. "You need to let me take care of you."

She glanced up at him, her eyes glistening with unshed tears. "All right. I'll meet with your therapist."

His heart pinched with the pain he saw in her expression. What he wouldn't do to take that hurt away, to kill and castrate the bastard that had put it there.

Zoe placed her head against his chest and let out a long, uneven sigh.

"It's going to be okay," he said tightly. It had to be. He couldn't lose her.

Jack stroked her hair and stared into the darkness. Acid burned in his throat when he looked back at the charred dresser. He needed to take care of this quickly—and there was only one person he knew could help her.

Jack cursed under his breath as he realized what he had to do.

Chapter 28

Zoe sat in Jack's car in front of a building on Park Avenue, while Jack's driver, Hands, stood impatiently by the open passenger door.

"I can't do this."

Hands' eyes darted up and down the street. "I can't keep you safe, out in the open like this. Get into the building. Quickly."

"This is Park Avenue, right? My insurance won't cover this. Take me home, okay?" A line of cars began to pile up behind their idling car. From the sound of their honking, people were getting impatient.

"Mr. Fialko will take care of you, Miss Burton. C'mon now. Be brave." He gently pulled at her elbow to where a uniformed door attendant stood and opened the door for them.

The attendant's kind eyes crinkled, "Give your name at the front desk, Miss."

She managed to mumble a thank you.

Her mouth fell open and she stared in astonishment at the elegant foyer. She swore the gilded room was more lavish than the famous Waldorf Astoria. The walls were upholstered, the floors polished marble. Four ionic columns held up a ceiling which loomed miles overhead. She would pivot on her heel and run like hell if it wasn't for Jack's driver. Sure, she needed to get the bad dreams under control, but not here. Not this way. What was Jack thinking?

An impeccably dressed lobby attendant sat at a deep mahogany desk. He eyed her up and down with an imperious sneer. "Can I help you?"

Her brain had shut down somewhere halfway across the lobby. She reached deep into her pocket and pulled out the wrinkled card. "Room two-oh-two. Doctor Framingham."

Nodding, as if the room number explained everything, the attendant had her sign into a gold leafed notebook using a heavy silver pen. He texted into his computer and pointed towards the elevators.

A pristine carpet runner led to a polished brass elevator bay. She pressed the up arrow. Two women waited alongside her. Their handbags had that familiar Gucci pattern and their clothes, no doubt, were designer, too. Both women were topped with perfectly coiffed, platinum blonde hair.

Zoe glanced down at her jeans and hoodie, embarrassed at how underdressed she was in comparison.

The elevator doors pinged opened and she crossed the long hallway over the marble parquet floor. She stood for the longest time staring at the oak door with gold lettering that proclaimed the occupant, *Dr. Diane Framingham.* Taking a deep breath, she pressed a button, waited for the lock cylinders to click, and let herself in.

Seeing no one, she sat down in a plush white leather couch. Wooden flutes with ocean sounds played in the background from a speaker in the ceiling. Tasteful framed original art of ocean scenes and seagulls graced the walls. Oversized leather furniture was placed around the room to minimize eye contact. The place screamed, *this is a therapist's sitting room for rich, crazy people.*

Her eyes watered when she thought of her own doctor, downtown. His waiting room contained blue plastic chairs and an old worn brown corduroy-covered couch, the floors covered with faded blue, industrial grade carpet. She could look up anytime, while waiting for him, and count the dots on the stained drop ceiling. Damn Jack for ruining everything. She wanted her old doctor back. Doctor Larry fit her like a worn-in pair of jeans. This one was like wearing five-inch heels, one size too small.

A woman opened the door and smiled sweetly. She looked like Scarlett Johansson on the cover of Vanity Fair. She had long legs, perfect blond hair coiled at her neck, and flawless alabaster skin. Zoe hated her immediately, yet managed to flash a saccharine-sweet smile right back at her.

"Zoe, right? Jack's friend? Please, come in." The doctor motioned her into a small room with subdued lighting.

It took a moment for Zoe's eyes to adjust.

Friend? He said they were only friends? Whatever happened to mate?

Calm down. I'm reading way too much into this.

The doctor pointed towards the couch. "Would you be more comfortable there?"

"No, I think I'll sit." She flopped down in a chair, eye to eye with the doctor. She crossed her arms across her chest.

The woman pursed her lips. "Of course, dear, please do. How about we just chat for a moment, and get to know one another?"

Oh hell, this was not going to end well. Zoe leaned back into the chair, maintained eye contact, and tried not to grit her teeth.

"Let's start on similar ground. How do you know Jack?" The woman spoke way too pleasantly and watched Zoe's face far too intently.

"He's my mate," She blurted out, feeling a smug sense of satisfaction when the therapist's eyes went wide.

"Surely you're mistaken." She looked Zoe over from head to toe, much like people viewed Nan with her tattoos. Horror and revulsion flashed across the woman's picture perfect face. A condescending sneer appeared briefly and faded just as fast.

"Don't think I could be mistaken about that, do you?" She'd had enough of Miss Prissy-witch.

"But, Jack is...I mean..." The doctor stood and closed the office door, putting her back to Zoe and tried unsuccessfully to regain her composure. "We all assumed he was too powerful. That he was eventually going to settle for a love match."

"Is there a problem that I should know about?" Zoe clenched and unclenched her fists. What was this woman's problem?

"I'm just curious. Where are you from? What clan?" Doctor Framingham stayed on the other side of the room.

"What does that have to do with anything?"

The woman was practically in tears. Slowly, she crossed the room and sat down heavily in her black leather chair. Her face had gone ashen and her lower lip trembled.

Shit, this was certainly not going as planned.

"I'm sorry. This is totally inappropriate. Of course I won't bill you. Please go." Doctor Framingham waved her hand at her, indicating she was dismissed.

No way. She wasn't going anywhere until the woman explained herself. Zoe had a bad feeling she knew where this was going, but she needed to hear it for herself.

"Are you and Jack, like, a thing?" She held her breath. *Was Jack playing the field behind her back?*

"We hook up occasionally. On and off. I just always thought, we might, well, get back together, eventually." The woman's eyes watered and her breath came in a little hiccup. "When he called me about you, I thought he had forgiven me, and he was willing to try again. I had no idea–"

She didn't need to hear the rest. *What the fuck? What was all that bullshit about mating for life?*

Zoe got slowly to her feet. She felt stiff, old, completely worn out.

Damn him all to hell. She was a fool for ever believing she could trust him, or anyone for that matter.

She'd been right about him, and about all men. They took what they wanted and left a shattered shell in their wake. Jack used women for sex, spit them out in tiny pieces, and left them bereft, and in her case, pregnant.

Crushing sadness replaced her initial anger.

She walked stiffly to the elevator. Her entire body had gone numb. Jack's chauffer would be waiting in the lobby. What was she going to do? She couldn't go back to Jack's apartment. Not yet, not until she'd processed everything. Without a second thought, she turned on her heals and found the stairwell.

By the time she reached the lobby, tears she hadn't even known she had formed wet trails down her cheeks. She brushed them away roughly. Seeing Hands pacing by the elevator bay, she darted across the atrium and pushed through the heavy doors.

She hailed the first cab she saw and jumped in, giving the driver the directions to Nan's apartment. Pulling her hood over her head, she crumpled back against the torn faux leather seat. Drawing a deep breath, she clenched her teeth and pushed back the sob that threatened to escape her throat.

Self-disgust filled her, burning a path straight to her soul. Never again. She'd promised herself to never let a man hurt her. And yet she'd trusted him. Given herself to him. In return, he'd tossed his ex-lover in her face. Worse, he'd expected her to share her deepest, darkest nightmares with a woman he uses to fuck.

Something inside her shattered at the realization. She might be screwed up, but she wasn't a doormat. Her stomach clenched and anger lashed through her. She'd been a fool to think Jack cared about her. She wouldn't make the same mistake again.

A small zap of energy shot out of her palms, and shot through the passenger seat in front of her, creating a small bullet size hole.

"What the fuck, lady?" The driver screeched to a halt, and pointed at the door. "Out."

"I'm sorry." She handed the man a twenty. He sped off before she had the chance to shut the door.

A shiver raced down her spine. If she'd been sitting in the opposite seat, the driver would have been dead. She pulled her hood tighter around her face.

You're broken. No matter how hard she tried to feel otherwise, she always came back to that one single truth.

Chapter 29

Sitting in Nan's apartment, Zoe picked up her phone, and scrolled through Jack's texts, before powering it off completely. Let him worry. She didn't care anymore. At least that was what she was going to tell herself until it became the truth.

She gave a weary sigh and curled up on Nan's bed, afraid to close her eyes. What if she had another nightmare? She wasn't just a risk to herself, but to everyone around her. Numb to everything except the constant pounding in her skull, she stared up at the ceiling.

A small noise came from the kitchen. She froze. Another creak, and a shadow crossed the hallway wall.

Someone was in Nan's apartment.

The hard rush of adrenaline rushed through her system. She conjured a small vortex of fire and let it hover in front of her. Carefully, she followed the sounds out towards the living room. She tried to adjust the intensity of the vortex so it was strong but not lethal. Taking a deep breath, she blindly threw the energy into the room.

The shadow dropped to the ground, panting.

She conjured more energy and was about to fire it when Jack's voice echoed through the darkness. "Zoe, stop."

Her fingers curled to extinguish the energy, but after a second thought, she let the vortex fly, hitting its target square in the chest.

Jack buckled over and groaned.

"What the hell are you doing here, Fialko?" She flicked the light switch.

He caught his breath and grinned. "Sucking in your essence."

"I want you to leave." Zoe clenched her hands into fists, ready for another blow. It had felt good to blast him.

Jack raised his eyebrows and held up a hand in supplication.

"Why are you here?"

He stood, shook off the effects of her blast, and crossed the room. "Diane called me."

"That's supposed to make me feel better?" She hissed in a breath when a fresh bout of anger gripped her throat.

"I'm sorry." He reached for her hand.

"Sorry?" She shook off his grip with a sharp motion, which caused a frigid breeze to blow through the small kitchen.

"What do you want me to say?"

"I don't know Jack. Figure it out for yourself. I got enough problems of my own without adding yours to the list."

"Diane said you were pretty upset."

She gave a small, tight laugh, and tried to stay calm, but all she could see was Jack hooking up with the picture-perfect doctor. His hands slipping through her perfect, platinum hair.

"Did she mention how she was the one who broke down in tears?"

"No." He winced. "She didn't."

"Did you even think about how finding out about us might hurt her? Hurt me?" Zoe's eyes began to water and she squished them shut. *Not going to cry.*

"Hurt her? No. I didn't." Jack eyes went hard, his voice clipped and tight. "She was the one that left me. Did she tell you that? I loved her. I was ready to stop searching for a mate that matched me, and marry her. Damn it, I was going to give up my clan's hope for the future for her. She dropped me like a bad habit during the last solstice and fucked herself silly with some other guy." His eyes sparked with fire and glowed briefly. "Why the hell would *she* care that *I* found a solstice mate?"

His words hit her like a blow to the gut. She sunk onto the couch, physically and emotionally numb, unable to breathe.

Jack had loved the ice princess doctor and he didn't love her. She gripped her queasy stomach and gave up hope of ever finding peace with her mate.

"You need to leave." Zoe couldn't even look at him.

"We've already had this discussion. You're *my* mate, carrying *my* child. I don't care how fucking angry you are, you come home with me. Now."

She glanced up at him. A hysterical laugh played on her lips. She finally understood what it was all about.

"You wanted revenge." She was such an idiot. Tears burned at the back of her eyes, but she refused to give him the satisfaction of seeing them. "You wanted to show her you had found a mate."

"That's ridiculous." Jack's face darkened with anger. "You needed a therapist and she's a good one. I was trying to take care of you."

"Bullshit." She stood and wrapped her arms protectively around her chest. "You had to know what was going to happen when the two of us met. When you said you found me a therapist, I really thought you understood, that you cared, but all you were doing was getting a bit of revenge on an ex. It's always all about you, isn't it? Do you even know how to care about someone else?"

"I do care about you," he said icily.

"No, you lust after me." She swallowed tightly, and gathered the strength for what she had to do. "Get out. I've had enough."

"I'm not leaving you. You're the mother of my baby"– he swiped his hands through his hair– "I have a right to be here."

"I swear I'll make you." Zoe raised an arm and the electrons in the room rushed into her.

"Bring it on." He was no doubt waiting for her to give him a burst of her energy so they could end up in bed.

"No, not that way." She lowered her hand and picked up the phone. "I'll call Olivia, Josh, get your whole family involved if I have to. I'll tell them how you've treated me. I'll tell them all how you sent me to Diane."

He scowled, his face dark with anger. "You wouldn't dare."

"I would and you know they'd take my side." Zoe knew she had finally hit home. "If you want any part in this child's life then I suggest you leave now. We're through."

"I see it as a draw, angel… it's a fucking draw." Tiny red orbs glowed in the center of his eyes. "I've waited my whole life to find you, and you refuse to cut me any slack. Damn it. I'm not perfect. I was trying to do the right thing. I heard your dreams. You flamed my dresser. I was worried about you. You could've burned down the apartment with us in it. I thought you needed help. That's what's wrong with you. You won't take anything from me except my cock."

Her pulse roared in her ears. "Get out."

He stormed out and slammed the door behind him.

"Don't ever come back," she shouted, and then crumpled to the floor in tears. How had he turned everything around? It was always about him and his needs. She didn't need that in her life right now. How could the most powerful witch on the whole East Coast be so intolerably needy?

Chapter 30

Immediately after the words came out his mouth, Jack regretted it. His mate could be so infuriating, but he ached to have her back in his arms even before he'd slammed the door shut. He should turn around and apologize–but he knew better. They needed to cool off.

If she wanted space, he'd give it to her. But first he needed to make sure her safety was guaranteed. He picked up the phone, called his security, and then called his brother, Josh.

"I need some extra security on Zoe."

Josh exhaled noisily on the other end of the line. "What's going on?"

"Just do it."

"Out with it, bro. Don't make me come up to the big city and try to beat it out of you."

"Zoe's being difficult." Jack eased down into the front seat of his car and put his forehead to the steering wheel.

"Difficult? What the hell does that mean?"

"She won't move in with me. She won't take any help for the baby. In fact, she doesn't want anything to do with me."

"Whoa, that's not difficult, that's painful. I mean, basically, you guys should be on your honeymoon."

"That's not how she sees it." He pulled on the seat handle, stared up at the gray fabric on the car ceiling, and moaned. "I really fucked up."

"I keep forgetting she thinks she's normal."

"It's worse than that, Josh, seriously. She has issues from her childhood so I sent her to Diane."

His brother didn't say anything for a long while, then let out a long breath with a whoosh. "Shit. Even you should know better than that. What's wrong with you?"

"I don't know." His insides hurt like he was being turned inside out. "When I'm with Zoe, I'm not myself. She makes me crazy. Besides, Diane and I haven't been together for over a year. I really thought it would be okay, but she made Zoe think we were still hooking up."

"Diane was no doubt a great lay but she's always been a vindictive bitch.

"No shit." Jack squeezed his eyes shut and pinched the bridge of his nose.

"Zoe's different. You gotta treat her differently than the women you've hooked up with in the past. I got the sense she wouldn't leave you even if you weren't mated. Think. How many women would mate with a guy they didn't even know in order to save his family? You have to fix this."

"I don't know how." Jack put his car seat back into the upright position. "She's an emotional wreck. Said so herself. A walking, talking napalm bomb."

Josh exhaled. "How bad is it? I don't mean to pry, but a witch as powerful as her with emotional issues could be a serious problem."

Fuck, if he didn't already know that.

"She had a nightmare the other night and almost blew up the bedroom in her sleep."

"Shit."

Jack banged his head on the steering wheel. "I'm screwing everything up."

"Give her some space. If she doesn't come around, go caveman on her and drag her back down to the shore."

"Thanks for the advice," he said sarcastically. He pulled his car into traffic and shook his head. "Did you find anything out about the guy that ran me off the road?"

"He's Russian Mafia. That much we're sure of."

"Anything else?"

"Nothing firm, but if he really has the vortex, he has to be related to her." Josh cleared his throat. "Keep her safe and back off for a few days. Everything's going to work itself out."

"Easy for you to say. Your wife is probably already warming your bed."

"Sure is." He said something to his wife and she giggled. "My girl is always there for me. That's the reward at the end of this. Keep that in mind."

Jack hung up.

How was he going to give Zoe space when he was going out of his mind with worry? And with want. He headed in the direction of his office. He'd submerge himself in work. Exhausted, he wouldn't be able to think so much about her warm body beneath his. About them swimming together in the ocean. The smooth curve of her hip–his cock twitched and he grimaced. Two weeks. He'd give her that long. Then, come hell or high water, he was going caveman.

Chapter 31

Zoe spent the next few days in a fog. She managed to buy three smoke alarms and a fire extinguisher so she could sleep, and a new deadbolt for the door. No more taking chances on any late night visitors. She would take control of her life one step at a time.

After a long internal debate, she made an appointment with her therapist. Feeling better knowing she had just made some positive steps towards improving her mental health, she logged into Nan's computer and requested more projects from her boss. He had enough to keep her busy, but not saturated. She needed more.

She opened her private stash of client emails and requested a whole other kind of work. If she was going to be a single mother, she'd need the extra cash. There were lots of questionable jobs online and she finally found one that was up her alley.

The request was for a simple security breach. She supposed it was wrong, but large companies deserved whatever the small guy could dish out. A twinge of guilt impaled her as she wondered what Nan would say. But how was a woman without a college degree supposed to make ends meet? Besides, if she was caught she could say she thought the job was legit.

Once emails were exchanged, she let one program chug away and worked the others. She toggled off all forms of communication. When evening came, she opened the empty fridge and ordered Chinese. She checked her texts and missed calls.

Jack hadn't tried to contact her. She should have felt relief, but her throat tightened and her eyes blurred. Had she really thought he would fight for her?

There was a text from her therapist's office, with an opening that afternoon.

Smiling, knowing she wasn't heading to Park Avenue, she slipped on her crusty old sneakers and caught the E train to Fourteenth Street. She changed to the N line downtown.

She caught her breath and dashed into the dilapidated building, just in time.

"Zoe. Wonderful to see you. I thought you were still down at the shore." Doctor Larry rose, held her hand, and motioned to her to sit in her favorite overstuffed chair.

Zoe never felt comfortable on the couch. It made her feel too vulnerable.

"I came home early. I'm staying at Nan's while she's overseas."

"Did you have a nice time?" He looked over the rim of his glasses and shuffled some papers on his desk.

"Yes and no."

He smiled patiently and waited for her to continue.

"I met someone," she sighed. "We had something, or rather have something, but now it's all messed up."

The doctor settled back in his own leather chair and folded his hands in his lap.

Zoe recounted the last few weeks. She included most of what happened, while modifying the paranormal interactions.

"That sounds pretty normal for a woman your age."

"Yeah, I guess, but I'm not normal. I'll never be normal." *Now more than ever.*

"You like to say that a lot." His eyes pierced her.

"It's true."

"Is it?"

"I have issues." Zoe shifted uncomfortably. Issues didn't begin to describe how being abused as a kid affected her behavior.

He smiled patiently. "Are you worried about how he'll react if he finds out?"

"I told him about my past."

The doctor leaned forward, raised his eyebrows. "That's a first. How did that go?"

"He said he wished he could kill my father for me. Something about cutting his dick off."

Doctor Larry let out a very rare guffaw. "That's an encouraging response, don't you think?"

"I suppose so." Zoe frowned.

As Zoe left the building, she couldn't decide if she felt better or not.

Fighting for normalcy was a life or death assignment. If she couldn't find that balance, Jack was going to take what little bit of herself she had gained in the last few years. He'd eat her up whole and she'd be left like when she was as a child–a man's plaything and her body not her own.

Chapter 32

Jack sat amidst the stack of archived copies his assistant had delivered. Somewhere in this mess was the clue to Zoe's family of origin. He began to sort through the family trees, diaries, and hidden random websites. What a nightmare to try to disassemble.

It was just about midnight when Jack, on his third cup of coffee, found a computer hyperlink with an astounding revelation.

"Motherfucker," Jack muttered to himself. He found his phone under a pile of papers and glanced at the time as he dialed. It was almost two in the morning.

"Josh?"

"Do you know what time it is?" Josh bit out on the other end. "Honey, it's Jack. Go back to sleep." There was a creak and a shuffling of feet on the other end of the line. "Talk."

"I'm going to send you a picture. Circulate it. Send out a red alert to every clan member. We're on lockdown. No exceptions. Understand?"

"What's going on?"

"I know who Zoe's stalker is."

Chapter 33

Zoe stared at the blood on her underwear and sat down on the edge of the bed, legs trembling. She doubled over, her stomach cramping. She crawled over to the bathroom and retched.

Something was very wrong and she shivered.

What was she supposed to do? After almost two weeks without Jack, she'd just begun to settle back into some semblance of normal. She'd been able to go back and forth to her job, her workouts, and therapy. She knew Jack had her followed, but that was okay as long as they didn't interfere with her life.

Her crying jags were down to twice a day. Perhaps someday, she'd be able to think about Jack without falling into emotional quicksand.

She rinsed out her mouth and picked up her cell phone.

"Come on Olivia, pick up." Zoe leaned back against the side of the tub and put her cheek to the cool porcelain.

"Hey," Olivia's singsong voice echoed on the other end. "What's going on? Jack won't tell me anything, and–"

Zoe hissed, another round of cramps gripped her gut, and she put her head to her knees.

"Hey, are you okay?"

"Not really." Zoe scooted over to the toilet and waited to see if she would puke again. It was a wonder the human species survived if this was what pregnancy was like. "I'm bleeding and cramping. I think something's wrong."

"You need to get to a doctor right away." Olivia sounded worried and that frightened her more than anything else this morning. "I'm going to text you the number of an obstetrician. She's one of our own. Tell her who you are."

"Liv, I can't–"

"Zoe this isn't just about you. Stop being so damn stubborn." Olivia sighed and softened her voice. "Let me know as soon as you find out anything."

"I will."

When her stomach finally settled, Zoe called the number Olivia had sent her.

"I'm...Jack Fialko's..." Zoe cringed. "Solstice mate. I think something may be wrong with my pregnancy."

The woman was all about efficiency as she took her name and information. "Can Jack get you here right now?"

"He's working and I didn't want to disturb him." *That sounded plausible enough.*

The woman paused for a few minutes. "Can you get yourself to a cab?"

"Yes." She'd do whatever it took in order to not have to call Jack.

"Good. We'll see you soon. Come right into the office. We'll be waiting for you." The woman hung up abruptly.

Zoe Google'd the address and moaned. Park Avenue again. This time she dressed in a designer summer shift she'd stolen for a song from the thrift store.

Hands was waiting for her outside the building. She hadn't seen him since she'd dodged him at the therapists, and from the look on his face, he still hadn't forgiven her.

Zoe groaned. "Did Olivia call you?"

He nodded brusquely and opened the car door.

A faint sheen of sweat covered her body when another series of cramps hit her. Hands was beside her, helping her into the car. She gave him a grateful smile, but his lips tightened in response.

As he pulled into traffic, he frowned at her through the rearview mirror. "Jack will kill me when he finds out I didn't call him."

"He doesn't care," Zoe said, resting her head against the leather headrest.

Hands snorted. "Want my advice?"

Zoe attempted a smile. "Not really, but I bet you're going to give it to me anyway."

Hands darted in and out of lanes with amazing efficiency. "Yeah, I am. You two should talk it out. You look like crap and so does Jack. Anything that hurts that bad has gotta be love."

He didn't know how wrong he was.

"It's a little more complicated than that. We don't even know each other." Except in bed. She left that part out.

"He needs you."

"I know, I know. We mated for life. We can't ever be with anyone else again–" She sighed.

Hands drove in silence for a while, looking way too often in his rearview mirror.

"He's following me again, isn't he?"

He nodded grimly. "I lost him. Don't worry."

Her stomach cramped again and she closed her eyes.

Hand pulled up beside the now familiar Park Avenue address.

"Don't wait for me, these appointments take some time."

"No can do. Call me when you're done." He frowned, and looked over the rim of his dark sunglasses. "Not like last time."

She breezed into the same building where Diane had her office, signed her name with the same guard, and exited onto the fourth floor. From there, a receptionist ushered her into a small, tidy examination room and asked her to change into a paper gown.

Within minutes a lovely, if somewhat distraught, brown-skinned woman entered. "Hi Zoe. I'm Dr. Abrams."

Zoe squirmed. The paper on the examination table crinkled under her. She hated doctors, even pleasant and lovely ones.

The doctor smiled sweetly and indicated that Zoe should lie back. "Let's just take a look. Usually solstice pregnancies are very strong. I'll need to examine you."

The doctor pushed and prodded, and took all sorts of blood samples while Zoe lay on the very uncomfortable table. She began to worry more when the doctor left her alone for what seemed like forever.

A nurse came in with all smiles and started asking genealogical questions. Most, she couldn't answer. When she mentioned that she thought her grandmother was from the healing clan, the nurse lost her bedside manner for a moment and stared with her mouth open.

"You're a mixed breed?"

"I guess." Zoe frowned.

The woman lost her genteel professional demeanor. "That was the first thing you should have told us. Are you really that ignorant?"

She turned with a theatrical huff and slammed the door behind her.

Soon after, the doctor returned, frowning intensely.

A cool breeze blew out of nowhere and the lights dimmed.

"Should I be worried?" Zoe asked, when the doctor continued to frown down at a chart.

"Do you know how many documented cases there are of mixed breed solstice babies carrying to full term?" The woman's dark eyes held a hint of sympathy.

"No," Zoe answered honestly. The woman was scaring her.

"One." The doctor stared at her with her hands clenched and her mouth all skewed up. "You and Jack should've let us know immediately."

"But what about my birth, I must have been a mixed breed?"

"You seem to have left out a lot of details." The doctor pursed her lips and held up the clipboard holding the all-but-empty form. "Do you even know if you were the result of solstice?"

Zoe started to answer, then shut her mouth. She really didn't know anything. "I just assumed..."

"We have no idea what we're dealing with. We're checking you into the hospital right now." The doctor scribbled some notes and stood as if to leave.

"Wait. Am I going to lose my baby?"

"Everything looks to be fine at the moment." The doctor's grim face spoke the exact opposite of what she said aloud.

"Then why do I need to go to the hospital?"

"If you check out okay, they'll release you. Why don't you call Jack and let him know."

"No," Zoe said a little too loudly, and the woman's brows rose sharply. Zoe fidgeted with the paper gown. "I don't want to worry him. You know how he is. When I get home I can tell him in my own way."

The doctor looked uncomfortable. It had to be obvious that everything was not smooth in Fialko-land.

"Very well. I'm calling an ambulance to take you over. Just lay right here and we'll take care of everything."

Zoe nodded and rubbed her hand over her stomach. Her fingers trembled and her panic swelled in her chest. No matter how messed up her relationship was with Jack, she hadn't wanted any harm to come to their child.

It just hadn't seemed real. Until now.

Zoe closed her eyes and said a silent prayer.

Please, baby. Be all right.

Chapter 34

Ivar pulled the phone's distorting speaker away from his ear and cursed. Somehow his cousin knew he'd lost track of his niece.

"What do you have to say for yourself?" His cousin's voice simmered to a low, poisonous, scorn.

"Calm down, Gregor. I'll pick up her trail again. It's a minor setback."

"Bah. You are lucky I still have need of your seed, cousin. But you don't need all of your fingers to fuck a witch…"

Ivar shuddered. There could be no more excuses.

"My men say the witch is pregnant. Why didn't you tell me?"

"*Futu-te*. Matters not. It cannot take. She will lose it and we will find a closer match."

"And does Fialko have our talent now?"

Ivar cursed again. "I have called for my best men to take care of the problem."

"Make sure you do. No more fuck-ups. You should have taken care of her as I instructed, then Fialko and his people would not be an issue. Now we have the possibility of an all-out war with the American clan."

"She's looking for her long lost family. We will help her with that, no?"

"Ha. If only she knew. What do you suppose she will do when she finds out you're her father's brother? Her loving uncle?

"It is a good joke, is it not?" Ivar laughed without mirth, but perhaps he would manage to keep his fingers. "My niece is getting cagier, Gregor. It's not my fault she found help with the Iesco clan."

"You are wrong, Ivar. She has always been clever and you have underestimated her. I won't let this abomination continue. It has to end here. That vortex is ours and ours alone. Do you understand me?"

"Da. What we will do with another vortex in our line, eh? We will be rich beyond our dreams."

Ivar sighed and hung up the phone, relieved he didn't have to explain about the Afghani girl that he'd also lost to the East Coast clan.

Chapter 35

Zoe rolled onto her side, careful not to pull on her IV and reached for her phone. She'd been admitted for observation, but no one was giving her any clear answers. All she knew was that she was stuck in the hospital at least for the night.

The silence was driving her nuts.

Scrolling through her texts and voicemail, she frowned. No new messages. Olivia still hadn't returned her call, and she tried not to notice that Jack hadn't messaged either. She'd thought about calling him, but what good would it do? Olivia, Hands, or the doctor surely would have told him by now.

Fresh tears surfaced and she blinked them away. She was so emotional lately. She knew he was mad, but *she* would've called *him* if he was in the hospital.

She knew he was pissed off, but even if he didn't care about her, his concern for his baby had always been his primary focus.

What right did he have to be angry with her anyways?

Sure, she had trouble connecting with emotions, but at least she'd tried to show him she cared. Hadn't she given up everything to mate with him? Help protect his clan? He was the one that said that love wasn't involved in mating–the one holding back.

His last words echoed in her ears. *That's what's wrong with you. Zoe. You won't take anything from me except my cock.*

When had he ever offered her anything else? As soon as the thought raced through her mind, she knew she was wrong. He'd offered her a life. A family. Protection for both herself and their baby.

Could she really be angry at him for not loving her? It wasn't like love was a choice. Would she really have chosen a warrior witch to fall in love with if it was?

Her phone pinged with a new email notification. Zoe frowned when she read the subject line. It was a response from her post on the popular ancestry site.

"Very good to be meeting you, cousin Zoe. My name is Roxana. Our grandmothers were sisters. I would like to be speaking with you more, but maybe we should be finding a better way. The sister of our grandmother remembers well the letter she writes for you, so many years ago, and does cry in happiness that you are writing in email to her. She says that she has much to share for you. If you make phone number, we can talk soon."

At the end of the email was a phone number with a Romanian country code.

This time Zoe did burst into tears. It was all too much. She was overwhelmed and exhausted. Her hormones were playing tricks with her emotions. Even if she could see past the blur of tears, she was too tired to respond.

Zoe curled on her side and tried to numb herself to the chaos that was her life. Her phone remained silent when the sky turned from reds and oranges to the dark purples. The fluorescent light hummed above her. Noises outside her door jolted her awake just as she began to doze. It seemed as if she hadn't slept at all when a nurse tried to wake her to take her vital signs. God, she hated hospitals.

She moaned loudly. "What time is it?"

"Six." The nurse attached a cuff around her arm and stuck a thermometer in her mouth. "Can I get you anything?"

Zoe took the thermometer out her mouth. "About eight hours more sleep."

The nurse chuckled, finished taking her blood pressure, and stuck the thermometer firmly back under her tongue. "You're being released later this morning."

"Guess they didn't find anything too serious."

"The doctor will speak with you before you leave." The nurse gave nothing away in her face or demeanor.

She couldn't go back to sleep so she turned on her phone. There was a single text message from Olivia.

Glad you're okay.

Call Jack!

That wasn't going to happen.

Instead, she decided to try FaceTiming her new Romanian cousin.

The first call was dropped. Determined, she tried again and was rewarded.

"Alo?" A blurry, yellowed image of a teenage girl came on the screen.

"Hello. Roxanna?" Zoe spoke slowly. "This is your cousin, Zoe."

The girl squealed in delight. "I am so excited to be speaking with you. Please, wait. I get my great aunt who is living with me. My English is only so good, but I can be doing this."

Even with the poor video quality, Zoe could see her great aunt had tears glistening in her elderly eyes. The woman spoke and Roxanna translated, "She say she is so very glad to be meeting you. She is overcome with happiness."

Zoe smiled and nodded.

"She say she will send you a ticket and you must come see her or–" Roxanne chatted excitedly with the elderly woman. Suddenly her face dropped into a serious frown. "Or baby may be died."

Zoe sat up more fully in her hospital bed.

"Aren't you making baby?" The teenager looked back to the old woman for verification and nodded.

"Yes, but how did you know?"

"My grandmother knows things. She is ummm… most powerful healer." The girl gazed intently on the screen. "Cousin. You must come. Grandmother buys you a ticket. No tell anyone. Someone meet you at the airport of the JFK. No more internets. No more emails. Danger for you. You see? Grandmother says baby in danger. You are in much danger. I don't know how to translate for you. Bad men want your baby but baby may die without her help."

"How do you know all this?" Zoe went cold. What was going on?

"Bad men find you. Go now. Is no time. She fixes everything. No bring baby father. No trust warrior men. Understand? She says no to trust anyone. Come now. Hurry. About an hour we text your phone."

The connection broke and Zoe stared at the blank screen. *What the hell?* At a very witchy gut level, she knew her great aunt was right. Her baby was in trouble, but lie to Jack and his family? How could she do that? The old woman had said to trust no one.

Not knowing what to do next, she decided to stop putting off the inevitable and called Jack.

"Hi, Jack." It took an awful lot of effort to sound cheerful.

The phone went silent for a while and then he whispered, "It's good to hear your voice. I've missed you, angel."

Zoe's mouth went dry. Truth be told, she ached for him every day and cried nonstop without him. "Me too. Did I wake you?"

"No. I've been up all night. Waiting for you to call me." He sounded as miserable as she felt.

"I've uh…been in the hospital." She should've called him last night.

"I know. I'm not supposed to upset you. Can I come in?"

Startled, she looked to the door where his voice originated. He stood in silhouette, back-lit by the hallway lights. His suit was wrinkled, his shirt untucked, and a tie hung loose out of his pants pocket. He moved in closer. Dark circles lined his eyes, his hair stuck out all over the place. Despite all that, he was a cool drink in a desert of loneliness.

She pushed up on her elbows and ended the call. "They didn't tell me you were here. I thought…I don't know what I thought."

He grabbed a plastic chair, dragged it across the room, and reached for both her hands.

He whispered into the darkened room, "The doctors wouldn't tell me anything. I had to call Olivia." His eyes lingered on hers with a big open question mark. "Are you really okay? The baby?"

"We're okay." She squeezed his hand and tried to find a reassuring smile. She swallowed hard to hold back the tears burning her eyes.

"Thank God. I've been so worried." He buried his face in her hand.

They sat like that for the longest time. She couldn't believe she'd allowed herself to live without him so long. "I've missed you..."

"I know." His voice cracked. Was he crying?

It was too dark in the room to tell and her hands were wet from her own tears.

"I didn't mean it when I said I wanted you to leave me."

Jack struggled to put down the side rail, then sat on the edge of the bed and pulled her to his chest.

"I didn't mean any of it. I was just being stupid." She'd forgotten how he smelled of firewood and ocean. Being in his arms was like coming home. "I'm so sorry about everything. I really suck at relationships."

"No. I screwed up. I'm the ass. Diane's the only therapist I know and she's really good at what she does. I had no idea...I was worried about you but I handled it all wrong."

He pushed her hair off her face and kissed her tears away until he found her lips.

God, she'd missed his lips.

When they came up for air, she asked, "So where do we go from here?"

"What do you mean?" He frowned. "You're coming home with me. Where you belong."

Zoe stared at the dark dotted hospital ceiling and tried to group them into sets of five for counting.

"That's the problem, Jack. I don't belong. I buy my jeans and sweatshirts from a second hand store, and until the other night, I never had more than lip gloss on my face. Park Avenue people are picture perfect. Your family? Olivia? Diane? All picture perfect." She shook her head and blinked hard. "I'm a mess. When that woman said you were a thing–"

"*Were* is the operative word, angel. Were. We haven't been together for over a year now. She lied. That's where you're different." His eyes glowed with intensity in the semi-dark room. "It's not about the clothes and the stuff on the outside. It's who you are inside."

Just outside the door, nurses were changing shifts with hellos, goodnights, and status on patients. What a cluster-fuck. She was going to have to lie to him, too, to get to Romania and save the baby. He'd never let her travel alone and he couldn't come. They would know. They'd see his aura a mile away.

"You're thinking." He tilted her chin up with his thumb. "What's wrong?"

Zoe paused and counted fifty more dots on the ceiling before she whispered again into the silence of the dark hospital room. "You said you loved Diane…I want to be loved, too."

Jack moaned and hugged her tight. "I want that for us, too, angel. Don't give up on me."

Don't give up on me after I do what I have to do.

"We're good. Really. Could you do me a big favor?" She gave him a big smile and hoped he didn't catch that she was faking. Thankfully, the room was dark.

"Sure, Zoe, anything."

"Can you give me minute? I need to clean up a little. And can you get me just a small cup of coffee? Half decaf and half regular. Lots of cream. No sugar. And a donut?"

He searched her eyes, then nodded.

Oh God, he was never going to forgive her.

When he left, she opened the dresser, threw on her clothes, and peaked out the door. Sitting down the hall facing her room was Hands still wearing sunglasses. She had no idea if his eyes were on her door. He could be sleeping or highly alert.

In her darkened room, she spun a small vortex in her palm and prayed she could keep it under control. Inside, a small flame burned brightly. Wishing she had played more softball as a kid, she lobbed the tornado at the fire detector right over the nurses' station and hit it dead on.

I'm so sorry, Jack.

Water gushed and a few nurses screamed as water poured down onto their heads and into their computers. Sirens wailed and red lights flashed. For that instant in time, Hands turned his head away from her door. She used the opportunity to dash down the hall and into the emergency stairwell. More alarms sounded, but no one paid the extra noise any attention. She made it to the bottom floor, just as fire trucks arrived at the scene. In the chaos, it was almost too easy to scoot around them and hail a cab to the airport. She hoped that no one was hurt, but her baby's life was on the line.

A text popped up on her screen with a terminal and flight number. Zoe paid the cab driver in cash, and wondered about how she was going to travel without a passport. She was never this flaky, but she had this overwhelming urge to get on a plane, find her healing family, and fix the baby.

How long should she wait before giving up and going back home?

"This is crazy," she muttered.

A man bumped into her with his suitcase, almost knocking her off her feet. Apologizing profusely, he grabbed her hand and thrust a small purse under her arm. She felt a jolt of healing energy and he ran off. She opened the purse and found a passport with her picture, money, and a plane ticket with a boarding pass.

She shook her head and wandered to her gate. The flight was already boarding.

What was she doing? There were so many things wrong with this situation, but she didn't have time to think.

She held her breath as she handed her passport to the agent in security. He glanced at the document and handed it back to her. "Have a good trip."

"Thank you." Her hands were shaking when she removed her shoes, her cellphone and her two purses into a container. When they called her flight, she looked down at her ticket for her row. She hadn't even noticed. She was flying first class to Europe and away from the man she loved, the father of her baby.

Chapter 36

Jack was in the hospital lobby when the alarm screeched. He dropped the stuffed animal, the Dunkin' Donuts tray, and bolted to the emergency stairs. On the eighth floor, he had to scoot past a tsunami of soggy hospital staff, gurneys, and wheelchairs before reaching Zoe's room.

Fuck. Her room was empty and Hands nowhere in sight.

How had he let this happen again?

Her last words haunted him. *I want to be loved, too.* What was wrong with him? Three stupid words. He'd fucked up again. He should have told her what she needed to hear.

Out of breath, Hands met in the hall, his clothes drenched. "Sorry. She was long gone by the time I made it to the street."

Jack bit back the scathing oaths at the tip of his tongue.

"Find her." Anger seethed in his low voice when he said, "And I want to know everything she's done for the last two weeks. Every call. Every keystroke. Everything. Are we clear?"

"Yes, boss."

An hour later, Jack sat in the back seat of the town car with a spreadsheet of every text and call she'd made in the last forty-eight hours. He cursed vehemently when he read the last few.

"Get us to JFK."

Hands grunted. The car slid in behind a line of taxis, went through a yellow light, and moved slowly along on Seventh Avenue South.

Jack keyed in Zoe's best friend's cell number and pressed send.

A concerned voice answered. "Zoe?"

"No. This is Jack Fialko."

"Fialko?" He could hear the frown in her voice.

"Zoe just bolted from her hospital. Did she call you?" Jack glanced out at the traffic as they crawled forward a foot at a time.

"Last time we spoke, she was pretty pissed off. Not sure if I'd tell you, even if I knew."

"You *are* aware she was kidnapped? Twice." Jack swallowed his impatience. Loyalty was one thing but Zoe and his baby were in danger.

"Hell no. The stalker?"

"Yeah. He's a hit man for the Russian mafia."

"Shit. Does she know?"

"I haven't had the chance. We've been, ah, apart." Jack cringed. Apart. Separated. Words he never wanted to use again.

Nan shot back. "The guy that's been after her for months is a *hit* man and you're waiting for the right time to tell her? What the fuck?"

"It's complicated." Everything about Zoe was complicated. They'd probably end up living separate lives, finding others to have meaningless sex. Frustrated forever.

Nan's volume increased a notch. "What do you need me to do?"

"Is it secure? To talk?" Jack scrubbed his hand over the stubble on his chin.

"This is the friggin' FBI. It's as safe as anywhere."

"The man who's been following her is her natural uncle. Her father's brother."

Nan whistled and the computer's speaker screeched. "Give me a minute."

There was a pause and he heard fingers flying across a keyboard. Some more clicks ensued, more pauses, and she muttered something he couldn't decipher.

"Shit. I swear, if anything happens to her, I'll kill you myself."

"No need. I'll do it for you." He turned up the volume so Hands could hear. "What did you find?"

"She has a new passport that matches a name on a manifest to Romania leaving in twenty minutes from JFK."

Jack cursed. "I'll never get there in time."

"I'm booking a flight to Romania as we speak. I'll meet you there–"

"Wait." Jack pinched the bridge of his nose and squeezed his eyes shut. Zoe would never forgive him if anything happened to Nan. "Do you have someone to watch your back? This guy is...powerful."

Nan gave a frustrated sigh. "I can handle myself."

"Did she tell you about my family's clan?"

"Of course," she snorted.

The car swerved, Hands cursed, and the side of a city bus almost clipped them. Jack gritted his teeth. "And?"

"There are more things in heaven and earth, Horatio..."

"You're quoting Hamlet?" He let out a little laugh. *What a strange woman.*

"Nothing like a good education and Netflix. I'll see you soon."

Jack hung up the phone and said to Hands dryly, "Nice driving."

His driver smirked, found an empty lane and barreled onto the entrance ramp for the FDR.

Romania. The home of her birth mother's healer clan. But why? There was only one reason. Jack called Olivia from his cell phone. "Hey."

"You find her?"

The black hole of the Brooklyn Battery loomed ahead. "I'm about to lose you. She's on her way to Bucharest."

"Romania?" Liv breathed out harshly. "Why?"

"Fuck if I know." He was whining and that fact sent him over the edge. He swore he'd never let a woman get to him like that again. "She didn't even tell me about the complications with her pregnancy. If she would have come to me and–"

"Really? Would you have honestly let her go off to Europe?"

"Hell no. The doctor said she needed to stay off her feet."

"You guys really have to work on your communication skills." She was cut off.

Jack swore and grumbled something unintelligible as he hung up the phone. His barely trained mate was on her own in another country, and running up against some of the strongest witches in the world. And it was all his fault.

Chapter 37

Zoe stumbled through customs and security in an exhausted daze, clutching her purse, and not quite knowing where to go. Most of the advertisements and airport directions she passed were in Romanian or Russian. She increased her pace and followed with the rest of the passengers through the main exit.

Families smiled and laughed, reunited. One by one, they exited with their suitcases in tow until she was the only one left from her flight. She desperately searched the crowd, not knowing who she was looking for.

"Don't look back. Walk quietly. One sound and I'll stick you."

She didn't need to turn around. His was the voice of nightmares. Finger-gun-man. *Didn't he ever give up?*

Zoe moved forward, while the tip of something very sharp cut into her back. This was *so* not going to happen again. Who the fuck did he think he was, threatening her and her baby? As her anger grew, the core center of her new talent flared and loaded like a sprung bow.

Electrons gathered, causing her hair to stand on end. She tried to hold onto her power but it had a mind of its own. Wind and fire burst forth. She prayed there would be something left of the airport.

This time, the fiery tornado was contained. It exploded almost inside finger-gun-man's head with a thunderous bang. He dropped his knife, fell to his knees, and both hands shot to his bleeding ears.

Behind Zoe, a slight woman screamed, "Bomba!"

From behind, a hand clasped hers tightly. Zoe spun around, ready to zap the person.

A teenage girl, with streaks of purple and pink in her jet-black hair pulled her in the direction of the door. "Come. Hurry. Car is there."

"Roxanne?"

The girl nodded and continued to tug on Zoe's arm. "We hurry. Now."

Zoe and the girl piled into the back of a small compact vehicle. Before Zoe could catch her breath, the airport fell behind and the screams of sirens faded away.

In the front passenger seat, a twenty-something woman with big brown eyes and dark hair, laughed nervously. "Good you have no luggage. I fear we would not all fit. I am Lana. You have met my sister-in-law, Roxanne, and the driver is my husband, Dirk."

The man gave her a small nod, then focused back on the road.

"We were very happy how well you get away from your uncle," Roxanne said, her eyes huge as she studied her.

"My uncle?" *Holy shit.* Zoe's mind raced. Her stalker was family. Bile rose in her throat when she remembered how he had unzipped his pants and almost raped her.

"Da, your father's brother." Lana's brows creased. "You did not know? When we get home, we will explain everything."

"Here. Eat." Roxanne pulled out a small meat sandwich from her handbag and handed it to Zoe.

Zoe mumbled a quick thanks and ate while the modern city of Bucharest rushed by outside the car window. She wished Jack was here with her. He would know the right things to say and do. She should have told him. It just all happened so fast and her great aunt had been so insistent. What a mess. The last few weeks had been miserable without him and now she'd made it worse. He was never going to understand or forgive her.

Once they left the city limits, Zoe tried to absorb the exotic countryside, full of forests and hills. The healers hummed a strange folk tune laced with healing energy, and she was lulled to sleep with dreams of a beautiful dark haired baby with a dimple in her smile. When she woke, the car was pulling into an old mansion built into the side of a hill. Deep pine forests graced the back of the building.

"Where are we?"

"Slobozia." Roxanne gave her a wide grin. "Our home."

"It's beautiful."

Fields of ferns and wild flowers crisscrossed the lawn in a beautiful spectrum of colors. Every shade of green on the face of the planet was represented in the huge garden. An enormous greenhouse stood to the side of the house, blooming with color.

Lana smiled, her love of the land, obvious. "Romania has some of the most ancient forests in the world, full of primeval plants with healing properties. With the internet, we send our seeds all over the world. Come, you must meet my Gram. You call her Bunica."

An ancient woman stood waiting at the top of a long and winding driveway. She opened the door and embraced Zoe in an enormous hug, overflowing with healing energy.

Lana translated her few words. "She gives thanks to the Goddess you are here, safely."

The two spoke again, and Lana's face lit up. "You are pregnant?"

Zoe nodded.

Roxanne danced around the car with a great big grin. "Bunica always knows when there is another life in the clan."

The old woman put a hand on Zoe's stomach. Instead of smiling, her mouth formed a large O. She stepped back, old eyes creased in pain, and made a healer's sign to ward off evil. Tears dripped in the corners of her eyes. "Why?"

Zoe looked to Lana. "Why what?"

Lana listened while the old woman ranted excitedly. When they finished their exchange, Lana turned to Zoe. "Why would you mate with a...a...Warrior?" She spoke the last word filled with contempt and disgust.

"We were pulled by the solstice." And because she was part warrior. Had she forgotten that, or just dismissed it?

Bunica cursed in Romanian. Zoe guessed at the meaning and started to get dizzy. She'd been up for almost two days straight.

"He raped you?" Lana motioned for her to sit down.

"No, no. He's not like that. I love him." Zoe sat, held her stomach.

"Tell me you did not match." Lana squatted beside her.

Zoe nodded miserably. "We have augmented each other's powers."

Lana interpreted for Bunica, her voice getting more and more agitated. Her hands went to her hips when she said, "So you have the wind tunnel from your father's side and what else?"

Zoe shrugged, held out a hand, and brought forth a small tornado with a raging fire burning within. She quickly put it out and sat on her hands.

The three women gasped, spoke simultaneously, and then nodded in agreement. What would they do with her now?

"We will save you from your evil mate," Lana said, nodding as if it were confirmed.

"What?" Zoe stood abruptly, and the room started to spin. "He's not evil. Tell everyone he's a good man. You must."

Zoe had to swallow hard. She closed her eyes and broke out in a cold sweat.

"No doubt this warrior has put you under his spell." Lana motioned for Zoe to sit down again, then patted her hand. "We will fix you."

Zoe let her head fall back onto the couch and closed her eyes. The world spun out of control. "No, no, he's a philanthropist... I keep telling you. A good man."

Lana stood, paced, and answered with anger. "Your uncle? The one who just tried to kidnap you? He pretends to be a good man. Zoe, the warring clan deals opium, and sells children into prostitution. They would sell their own mothers if there was profit in it. It is the warrior witch's way. They are warlocks. Liars."

"The men who are after me are my birth father's family? What do they want with me?" Zoe tried to think clearly. The odd time zone, the pregnancy, and the flight were making things worse.

"It is obvious, no?" Lana took a deep breath and spoke as if to an ignorant child. "Before you were even born, clan warriors were bartering for the right to try to mate with you, to have your father's power. That is why your parents tried to leave the country. They died in that effort. Somehow, you were lost. Now that you are with child, and have given yourself to another clan, they want the child you carry. And then, perhaps will want to seed you with one of their own."

"They want my baby?" Zoe moaned. When would this nightmare end? These people talked about pregnancy like she was a race horse.

Roxanne brought some refreshments into the room on an old silver tray.

Bunica spoke to Lana slowly, pointing her fingers at Zoe, in emphasis.

Lana nodded and translated "The wind power had only been in the Russian hands. They want that back, along with the fire that you have from your husband."

"We didn't marry," Zoe muttered miserably. She wouldn't trap him legally. It was bad enough they were trapped by mating.

Lana translated, and Bunica went off again.

"What is wrong with you Americans? You have baby, you get married. It is simple. Will he not give your baby his name and his honor or is it as I suspect, he raped you?"

"I love him." Tears had gathered in her eyes and she blinked them away.

The old woman answered back in a mixture of broken English and Romanian. "There is no love from a warring witch.

If you want love, you should have chosen to mate with the healing side of your nature. We understand the heart."

"It's too late. Will you help me keep my baby or not?" Zoe clenched her fingers into fists and tried to fight back the panic crawling up her skin.

"I must think. This time it may be better to let nature keep its course." The old lady paced back and forth across the parlor.

"But you helped my mother." She couldn't believe what she was hearing. After she'd traveled all this way?

"Our clan was going to use your mother's power to protect us from the Russian," Lana said, translating her grandmother's words again. "What good did that do?"

Bunica stared out a full picture window onto the vast gardens and was quiet for some time.

Zoe tried to plead again. "Please Bunica, I'll show you his family online. You can speak to Olivia, a Healer and his childhood friend. She'll speak for him. Things are different in the US. Please, I already love this baby and love her father. I cannot go on without them. I will not."

The old woman's face softened, but she smiled kindly for the first time. Her voice was gentle when she spoke again.

Lana translated. "She says cannot do this thing you ask without speaking to the rest of clan. For now we will keep you both safe. Go rest. We will meet with our clan this evening."

"Thank you." Zoe gave a small smile.

Lana led her up a graceful staircase, into a bedroom, and turned down the white comforter. She closed the heavy violet wool drapes, leaving the room almost completely dark.

Zoe sat down, took off her sneakers, and laid her head down on the pillow.

"You are a huge risk to the whole world." Lana pulled up the blankets, patted Zoe on the shoulder and sighed dramatically.

"I didn't plan this. It just happened."

"Go to sleep now," Lana stated quietly. "I'll wake you when it's time to go."

Chapter 38

Zoe walked up the aisle of the dingy gray auditorium, surrounded by her new family. Noisy clan members sat in well over two hundred metal folding chairs. Some pointed and stared, while others held heated discussions. What little she could translate did not bode well for her baby. She took a deep breath, slowly climbed three stage stairs, and took a seat next to Bunica on the podium.

After one of the witches gave a benediction, it was Bunica's turn. She spoke slowly so Lana could translate.

"So you see, I don't feel that a decision as great as allowing this baby to survive should rest solely on my shoulders." Bunica turned her back to the audience and nodded.

Zoe swallowed hard, coughed, and tried to unlock her fingers wrapped around her note cards. The microphone sat, waiting like a cobra with a skinny black stand for a body.

A middle-aged woman spoke up from the audience. "Have her show us what she can do."

Zoe looked at Bunica who gave her a small nod.

On trembling legs, Zoe stood and made her way to the podium. She raised a shaking palm, created a small tornado, and then extinguished it quickly. Many in the assembly gasped and several people made signs to ward off evil.

A large man with a potbelly stomach stood. "Why would we want more of that in the world?"

Zoe clenched both her trembling hands behind her back and leaned into the mic. Her voice boomed and she jumped. "The baby wouldn't be theirs. She'd be mine. She'd be raised in love. Surely you wouldn't deprive her, one of your own clan, at a chance at life?"

Another man stood. "I say just let nature take its course. Healer should never mix with warring. It's an abomination."

"So, is that what you all think of my worth, too?" Zoe glared. She raised her arms theatrically and summoned the wind. Her dark hair came out of its braid and three pieces whipped around her face like Medusa's snakes.

Several healers screamed and ran out of the hall.

"The baby's father's clan are good people. They are police officers, firefighters, doctors and psychiatrists. They are dedicated to making life better for healers and warriors alike." That sounded so lame and the faces out there totally agreed. She took a deep breath and prayed for strength, for the right words. "You need my mate's clan...my clan, to protect you from the Russians."

The crowd grumbled.

"I promise you, Jack Fialko comes from an old and noble family." She stood taller, and her voice lost its quiver. "Our joining is the will of the Goddess who rules us all."

What other words would convince? Her brain went blank, her cheeks burned, and a couple people in the audience cleared their throats in the silence. Sweat trickled down her sides and her body odor wreaked of failure.

How could she ever face Jack again? If their child died, it would be her fault.

It must have been the thought of him that caused the six inch vortex to appear before her.

No fire burned within it, just beautiful violet, sparkling, healing energy.

As it twirled into a long spiral, she closed her eyes and remembered. She poured all their hurts, their laughter, and their love into that vortex. Her gut wrenched and her throat constricted, but it wasn't enough. She added her childhood pain, her friendship with Nan, and finally the essence of her whole being. The vortex grew larger and intensified in spin and color. She sobbed. Never had she felt so alive, nor ached so much.

The spiral moved up into the center of the ceiling, crackling and humming like a top. The seated clan members gazed up with eyes and mouths open.

Without warning, the energy cloud exploded and tiny violet lights floated down onto the heads of all. For a moment, everyone's skin glowed with eerie lavender and then understanding filled their faces. When smiles and tears looked upon her, she knew they understood.

She closed her eyes and lifted up a silent prayer of thanksgiving. Her child would live. Zoe's heart clenched with relief.

Zoe started back to her seat, then froze. She hadn't sensed him until that moment, but there was no denying the sensations that wrapped around her, drawing her attention like a magnet. In the far corner of the auditorium, hidden in the shadows, was the man she loved.

Chapter 39

Jack stood with Nan, listening to his mate's plea for their unborn and his heart had swelled with pride. He'd started for her when she'd panicked, but stopped when the vortex had appeared. When a piece of her light hit him, he leaned against the wall, gasping for a breath. Never in a thousand years would he have guessed the intensity of her feelings. The damnedest thing was, perhaps due to lack of oxygen, in that moment the fog cleared.

He'd been such an idiot.

His chest clenched. He loved her. There was no denying it any longer. She wasn't just his mate. She was his heart.

He stepped into the middle of the room. There was a collective gasp, but his gaze stayed steady on the only person who mattered—his Zoe.

"I'm Lord John Makepeace Fialko, principal of the American East Coast Iesco clan. Whatever assurances you need from my clan, I will fulfill. I too, beg for my child's life. My clan will owe you. We always pay our debts." He turned slowly and met the eyes of the crowd. "If you do not, I will be a revengeful adversary."

"What good will your protection be, Fialko, if we're all dead?" said a wiry nervous man near the back.

"My family protects its own." Jack stepped further into the room. "When Zoe mated with me, you all became my family. When the baby is born, I will be bound to you by blood. I will honor that blood with the blood of my clan."

The crowd gasped at his bold oath. What was he doing? He had all but declared war on the Russian mafia.

An ancient woman stepped forward from where she was sitting on the makeshift podium, "We are honored, Jack Makepeace Fialko, leader of the Iesco clan, to accept your protection. In turn, our clan will provide healing and comfort from now until the twilight of time to you and yours. Welcome little brother." Like a grand queen, she glared out into the audience. "Are we all in agreement?"

From the back of the room, Nan put her hands together in a single clap, and one by one everyone joined in. Jack sighed. Damned if he knew how he would keep his new family safe from halfway across the world, but he'd deal with the fallout later. All that mattered was that Zoe and his child were safe.

Nan ran to the front of the room, jumped onto the stage, and embraced his beautiful, courageous mate.

He walked slowly up the aisle, allowing Zoe time with her friend, but he was aware that her gaze kept flickering to him.

A small hum of an ancient Romanian tune started somewhere in the middle of the group which others took up. A few guitars joined in with tambourines and singing. Chairs were folded and moved to the side. Soon the whole group was singing and dancing somewhere in-between a modern club and an old gypsy camp.

The sound echoed eerily in the old building.

Zoe touched Nan's arm, whispered something in her ear, then walked slowly towards him. She licked her lips nervously as she approached.

"I'm sorry for not telling you," she said, not meeting his gaze.

"Never leave me again, angel." Jack reached out and brushed his thumb over her cheek.

Tears gathered in her eyes and spilled down her cheeks. "I won't. I promise."

Relief flooded through him. He wrapped his arms around her delicate shoulders and pulled her against his chest. Damn, he'd missed her. He smiled when her eyes widened at his arousal.

He ached to take her back to the hotel, but there was still unfinished business. "I am expected to form alliances, and we need to dance with your clan to seal the deal."

Zoe frowned and glanced around at the crowd who were now mostly gathered in the center of the auditorium, hopping and skipping to an unfamiliar Romanian folksong.

"I don't dance." She clung to him and his heart burst. Even if they never had children, she would be his water in the desert forever.

Jack let out a low chuckle and lifted a brow. "Not even heathen humping?"

She hit him lightly on the shoulder and smiled. "It's called Zumba."

He nuzzled her neck, and moved to the beat of the music. She relaxed and let him lead.

"I'm sorry I didn't ask you to come."

"And I'm sorry about everything, Zoe." He gave her a little grin and held his breath. "Will you marry me?"

She glanced up at him and her eyes went huge, and he saw a spark of hope. Then just as suddenly, a shadow fell across her expression.

The music changed to a slow exotic beat and Jack used it to draw her even closer. Healing power pulsed into the room, like the aroma of an orchid, thick and overpowering.

"You have to now, you know." He kissed her forehead and let his lips linger there, her skin warm and sweet. "Your old fashioned relatives will insist."

With a low, breathy voice, she said, "You're my mate, what do we need the license for?"

"I want it legal." He threaded his fingers through her hair, enjoying the silkiness. "I want to be the baby's father, and be your mate, in all ways, human and warrior."

"I want that too." Her eyes once again glimmered with hope. "I love you, Jack."

She was so beautiful that the words he had memorized got stuck in his throat. He dropped his hands from her side and tried to get it right. Before he could voice what he was feeling, he saw hurt flash across her face and she ran.

"Wait, Zoe! Dammit, come back."

Suddenly the florescent lights in the auditorium went dark.

Zoe stopped running and looked around in confusion. Without thinking, Jack summoned a vortex, stepped in, and dashed towards her. He grabbed her around the waist and pulled her to his chest.

"Give yourself up, Fialko, along with that half-breed witch or I start shooting." The voice sounded way too close.

Zoe tensed and he drew her closer.

"No need. I am here. You're the one hiding in the dark like a cockroach."

There was some small rustling and then the lights came back on. The healers backed away to the sides of the auditorium, leaving two vortexes in the center. The Russian was barely visible, azure energy swirling around him like a gaseous planet, but Jack could see enough to know that the man wasn't Zoe's stalker.

Lord Gregor Uragan stood before them, his full lips drawn up in a scowl. "It's too bad, but I have to kill you now, Fialko. The vortex, I cannot allow you to have it. You see how it is. Nothing personal, my friend."

Jack calculated the odds of getting out alive, with no one getting hurt, and it wasn't good. At least twenty of Gregor's men mingled among the grim-faced healers.

"Maybe we should take this outside," Jack snarled, fury snapping through his body. "You're going to need your healers alive when I'm through with you."

"Perhaps first, I kill the meddling old woman." He raised his arm towards the healer leader, a crazed smile on his lips.

Before Jack could stop her, Zoe's arm shot out and she blasted a small fireball at Uragan. The bullet-like vortex pierced through his shielding, and he screeched, cradling his arm.

"You little bitch," Gregor screamed in outrage.

Jack cursed and held her arms down. "Hold off, Zoe."

Gregor's face twisted in a hideous scowl. "You see why I can't allow you to keep her, my friend?"

"You have to let me go with them," Zoe whispered, her expression frantic. "I won't have all these people die for me. I won't have *you* die for me."

Gregor stepped closer. "Listen to the little lady. You just gave an oath to keep these sheep safe. One little explosive tornado would kill them all. Even you, Fialko, could not have perfected the combination of powers yet."

Fear lanced through Jack's system. The swine was right. He'd been too busy trying to keep Zoe safe to put time into practicing with his new power.

"Let me go with him, Jack." Zoe squirmed in his grasp.

"No." He gripped her midsection tighter to emphasize his point.

"I won't sit here all day, children, while you argue. I will start killing, starting with the translator." Gregor cackled and conjured a ball of energy.

Before he could stop her, Zoe fired a tornado that sent Gregor sprawling to the back wall.

"Zoe." He tried to keep his arms wrapped around her, but her energy pushed him away.

One by one, she blasted each of the Russian warriors, dead center, with surprising accuracy.

Jack maintained their shield, using all his power to block the Russians' retaliation.

Zoe's shots were amazingly precise. Unlike him, she could tell from their auras, which were warring. The few Russian clan members still standing, grabbed the fallen, and left the auditorium cursing.

Jack dropped the vortex. Zoe's legs gave out and she collapsed against him.

The ancient leader rushed over to Zoe, laid hands on where her child grew within, and nodded with a half-smile. "No too sick. Understand? We go."

Cradling Zoe in his arms, Jack carried her to a waiting van. It wasn't until the buildings faded to deep pines that Jack spoke again. "Something's wrong with her."

The old woman reached over the front seat, frowned, and spoke to the driver in Romanian. He sped up, and the younger woman who was introduced as Lana, interpreted. "She asks why you let your woman fight your battles?"

"She doesn't listen. I was going to negotiate." Jack gritted his teeth to hold back the curse on the tip of his tongue.

"The Russians don't negotiate, Lord Fialko." Lana shook her head in disgust.

"They will or they'll die. Honestly, after tonight, I'm not sure if I really care."

Lana translated and the old woman grinned in approval.

The driver spoke excitedly in Romanian and pointed to the rear window.

"They haven't given up," Lana said, nodding behind them.

Jack swore. *What the hell was wrong with these guys? Didn't they know how to say uncle?*

Lana seemed to read his mind. "They need us. They have injured men and we are their only healers."

Jack twisted so he could keep one eye on the car following and one on his sleeping mate. He smoothed the hair from her forehead. What an amazing woman. Blending talents was a huge challenge, even for the most skilled. How had she managed to get so good, so fast?

They drove up a long driveway. The facade of a small cottage hid a much larger building behind that spread long and wide under enormous pines. When the car stopped, the ancient healer motioned that Zoe should be taken from the car.

Reluctantly, Jack allowed one of the male healers to take Zoe from his arms.

"Go with her," Jack said to Nan.

Nan nodded and followed them into the house.

Lana translated, "She asks what is your wish? Because you have claimed us, we are under no obligation to heal the Russian injuries. She prefers to let them die."

"Zoe was the first to fire," Jack said, giving them both a scathing look. "I won't subject her to global court."

More cars pulled up the long driveway. Jack summoned a small fire-vortex as a warning and willed his arm not to shake. The last fight had left him exhausted. He hoped the few standing wouldn't call his bluff.

A warrior threw a cell phone at Jack. "It's Lord Uragan for you."

"What are your terms, Fialko?" Gregor spit out his name like an insult.

Jack ignored the tone. "Agree to speak with me, alone, and I'll let my new healers work on your men."

"Done."

"Not so fast. I need a temporary truce until we reach an agreement." A line of over twenty cars lined the driveway and more were arriving, parking along the road.

Gregor muttered an acceptance of the terms and hung up.

Jack motioned to the healer leader with a wave of the hand. The injured were dragged and carried through the front door. The crisis was put on hold, and Jack raced into the main house to find Zoe. She was sitting up on a small couch in the living room, sipping tea.

"Are you okay?" He wiped the sweat dripping off his brow, sat down, and held her until his racing heart stilled.

"I'm fine." With two palms to his chest, she pushed him away and spoke with a chill in her voice. "What's going on out there?"

What had he done wrong now?

"Your family is healing the injured. When they're finished I'll negotiate a treaty."

"Another one of those warrior clan things, I suppose." Her eyes refused to meet his and her frigid tone sent chills down his spine.

"You're going to have to learn some of these rules. You're lucky I'm not taking you to Berlin for a hearing of the global court." He cringed at the harsh words. He'd meant to say something reassuring and sweet. Something to make the stars shine in her eyes.

"No more lectures." She lay down on the couch and turned her back to him.

It came to him like a slap across the face. She'd told him she loved him, but like a fool he had hesitated.

"Zoe, the lights went out before I could explain how I feel." Jack went to his knees beside the couch.

"It's easy enough." She turned with her big sad eyes just inches from his. Tears pooled down the sides of her face and her voice cracked. "I say I love you, then you say, I love you, too. Unless you don't."

"But I do, angel." Jack cupped her cheeks in his hands. "That's what I've been trying to say. Love doesn't even begin to cover how I feel and that's why I hesitated. I've loved you since the moment I first saw you in Olivia's shop. I just didn't want to admit it."

Her eyes went wide, softened, and her gaze fell to his lips. "Really?"

"I love you, Zoe." He brushed his lips against her. "I can't live another day without you. You're everything in the world to me."

A fresh surge of tears welled in her eyes. "I love you too."

Her fingers dug into his hair and she devoured his mouth. The addictive taste of her infused his senses. She was safe and so was their child.

Everything was going to be all right.

"Russian whore."

Shit. Jack jumped back.

Ivar Sokol, Zoe's stalker-uncle stood in the doorway. The little bit of flesh showing under his bandages was bubbled and burned. His eyes burned wild with insanity in the instant before black poisonous energy shot out from his hand.

Jack went down hard, unable to move. Every cell in his body cried for death instead of gut-wrenching pain.

"You fucking bitch." Ivar limped across the room, raised his hand, and summoned another vortex.

Zoe screamed, Jack moaned, and a gunshot exploded.

A red hole the size of a penny appeared in the forehead of Ivar's stunned face. He crashed back onto a glass coffee table.

Nan rushed to Jack's side and put two fingers to his neck, checking his pulse.

"Fialko? Are you alright?" Nan asked, keeping her back to him and her weapon trained on the door.

A sparkling vortex materialized and spun over their head. It sliced through Jack with excruciating pain, sucked out the darkness of Ivar's shot, and relief followed.

Nan's eyes went wide. "Holy fuck."

For a while, all three just stood, staring, and processing.

Jack exhaled, moved his limbs, and when he could, sat up with his back to the couch. Zoe's hand reached down and he put it to his lips.

"I had no idea he'd try that again." He glanced at Nan. "Thanks."

"No problem." Nan grinned and scratched her chin. "I'll probably get some damn award for shooting him. That guy's wanted by Interpol."

"Still, I owe you." Jack grinned back and scrambled off the floor before the pooling blood reached him.

"I'll collect when we get back to the states. What I wouldn't do to have just a little of what you can do." Nan's eyes went to the ceiling as if something still lingered. She opened her cell and walked to the back of the room.

Jack glanced at the time. Gregor Uragan and his men would be arriving shortly.

"I want you to stay in the house while I speak to Gregor."

"No way." Zoe stood, and smoothed her dress down. Her hands pulled out her hair tie and made a neat ponytail. "I'm coming with you. If he tries anything–"

"I'm not putting you or our baby at risk again." Jack wobbled. That probably wasn't his most commanding performance.

She steadied him and put her arm around his waist. "I don't want to put you at risk, either."

"All right." He placed his forehead against hers and breathed in her scent. "As long as you do as I say, and no trying to blast them into tiny pieces." He pulled back and gave her what he hoped was a stern look. "Understand? We're not going to start a clan war."

"But isn't that what they were doing?" She walked him to the back door. Gregor was already by the cottage door, barking out orders.

"Yes, but not formally. That's the trick. If I use our clan laws, they'll be bound."

"They have no morals." Zoe scrunched her eyebrows and frowned. "Better to blast them now before they can do any more harm."

He stopped and gripped her shoulders. "Our ancestors made complex rules around treaties and the magic that binds it."

"Worse than mating during solstice?"

He chuckled. "Much worse. It could take centuries to resolve this properly."

"Centuries?" Zoe glowered when they approached the Russian leader, and whispered under her breath. "I still think it's easier to just blast them."

He took her hand and gave a little blast of energy to silence her. She looked up at him with a pout, then smiled. The air around them stirred and his senses opened. It was all he could do not to kiss her.

She owned every part of his body, heart and soul. And yet in that moment, he felt her relent, give up control. In her eyes, he saw it. She gave her trust to him completely and without hesitation. Every muscle, every nerve, and every cell in his body was infused with her love. There was no greater gift. No great power.

With the strength of his mate beside him, Jack turned to the powerful Russian warrior, made a quick nod, and held out his hand. "Lord Uragan, my clan has over fifty treaties currently in negotiation. Yours will make fifty one."

Epilogue

Jack glanced into the bassinet, unable to stop staring at the sleeping baby. He'd been waiting for her eyes to open for at least an hour, but like her mother, she was stubborn. He stroked her tiny fingers and contemplated the miracle. He still couldn't believe how lucky he was.

"Don't wake her up." Zoe curled an arm around his waist. Her voice scolded but her eyes sparkled under the fake frown.

"I wasn't going to. She's just so amazing." He rested his arm over Zoe's shoulder and smiled.

How far they'd come. He had two angels to care for now. How had he ever survived without them? He couldn't even remember.

Cecille stirred with a little whimper and immediately he lifted her out of the crib. He had no idea babies would be so demanding or smell so sweet.

Zoe poked him in the side and whispered, "She doesn't need to eat for another hour. Let her be."

"I just want to hold her for a minute." Cecille's head fit into the palm of his hand, and her body barely reached the length of his arm. Her mouth made a sucking sound, but her eyes stayed closed.

"If you put her back down, I can think of something more interesting to do." Zoe nibbled an ear.

Jack raised his eyebrows. "So soon?"

"You want to be celibate the rest of your life?" She unbuttoned the top button of his jeans and he hardened immediately. Two months had never seemed longer.

"No, but..."

"Neither do I." Zoe placed her hand on his abdomen, and conjured a vortex of fire and wind that caused his shirt to singe on the edges.

Oh dear God. He set the baby carefully back into the bassinet, then led his wife into the master bedroom.

"That was my favorite shirt."

"Oh well." She flashed a smile at him.

He smirked, conjured a small ball of energy, and disrobed her completely. "Bring it on."

Mated by Magic Book #2

Read More:
https://www.amazon.com/Dark-Tremor-Mated-Magic-Book-ebook/dp/B01DWIXD0K
Free on Kindle Unlimited

Chapter 1

Let's see what this baby can do. Jace revved the custom engine of his new ATV and grinned. The desert whirled by at 100 mph, he caught some air, and flew.

"Fuck yeah!" *What a rush.* Better than winning at the tables last night.

Back teeth chomped together when all four wheels landed. He turned the wheel in the opposite direction, rotated his wrists, and his ride sped forward. *Sweeeeet.* Ahead lay nothing but blue sky, a couple cactuses, and a lot of empty miles.

Above him a falcon circled, then swooped low. He only took his eyes off the terrain for a moment, but when he looked back, his vehicle rocketed full speed towards a woman's small form. With only a couple feet to spare, he cranked the wheel and held his breath.

Shit. Where the hell had she come from?

With each turn of the deathly merry-go-round, a huge boulder grew closer. Time stood still. Impact imminent. As he spun out, he swore a fissure ripped through the surface of the desert and the mammoth rock sank halfway into the riverbed.

What the fuck?

Another turn.

The blob disappeared.

His right front wheel hit something solid, and he flipped and rolled. A sickening crunch, followed by an odd silence, except for the spinning of tires.

With some effort, he unclenched his jaw and took a deep breath. The sharp edges of the harness dug into his neck and the sky stood where the ground should be. But he was alive.

Upside down, a woman, no, *the* woman who'd just caused this disaster peered down, or rather up, and said, "Are you okay?"

"Hell, no. I'm not okay, lady. Look at my ATV." *What a stupid question.* Adrenaline raced through his veins, needing an outlet.

Her face-load of attitude and army-surplus attire was covered in dust. "Listen to me, asshole. I don't give a shit about your vehicle. Were you hurt?"

He wiggled his toes. Good.

Fingers. Good.

Hanging like a bat, he wedged his legs and released his harness. The world righted itself when he jumped onto all fours and crawled out of the wreckage onto the cool morning sand.

"What the hell were you doing out there? I could've killed you." His hand came back bloody when he rubbed above his right eye.

"Me?" Her dirty brows furrowed. Blue eyes glared, white teeth showed, and no doubt, sharp claws hid inside the oversized jacket. "Didn't you see the no trespassing signs?"

"There weren't any signs," he growled, rolling his shoulders. A wave of nausea washed over him and his vision went foggy. He gripped the side of the ATV to keep from tumbling forward.

She rolled her eyes. "You *are* hurt. Follow me."

A sweet little ass turned and walked towards a nearby hill.

Before following, he tried to clear his thoughts and recall the sequence of events.

Woman. Bolder. And... *earthquake*? He hadn't imagined the two foot gash that zigzagged across the river bed. What were the odds?

Slim to none.

Suspicious, he followed her up a steep hill, and through the glassed-in front wall of some kind of cave dwelling. Figures. The badger had a burrow.

"You live in a cave?"

"Earthship. Entirely eco-friendly." She pointed to a ladder-back chair and threw him a roll of paper towels. "Sit and try not to bleed on anything. Give me a sec' to clean up."

While water ran from behind the bathroom door, he pulled off a wad of paper towels, and pressed it to one eye. With the other, he made a quick assessment of her space. Cheap, but sparkling appliances lined one wall. On the other side of the island that divided the open space, a lumpy couch faced a fourteen-inch screen.

Above, a wood railing circled a loft with a low bed.

He jumped when an orange tabby landed on the large antique table in front of the glass wall. It padded around a short wave radio and a laptop, making a dreadful meowing sound. It sat down next to a pile of rough, blue stones.

Jace picked one up and whistled through his teeth.

Turquoise. Beautifully veined. And not from a mine he recognized. Probably worth a small fortune.

Wet-faced, she dashed out of the bathroom with a towel around her neck. "Put that down."

The gem fell from his hand and his mouth dropped open. *Holy hell.*

Her newly scrubbed face revealed a pert nose and wide kissable lips, framed by long dark-blonde hair. But it was the damp white t-shirt, worn without a bra, leaving little to the imagination that had his cock standing at attention.

When she caught him staring, she turned bright red and grabbed a sweatshirt off a chair. It was too late. His dick knew what it saw—and it wanted it.

Bustling across the room, she struggled with her zipper while trying to balance a first aid kit under her arm.

"I said not to touch anything." She picked up the stone and put it back in the pile.

"Sorry." Arms raised, he stepped away, but couldn't hide the widening smirk.

"Sit down and I'll clean your cut." Small palms pushed at his chest ineffectively, but remained, as if glued. She stared, stunned.

The energy pulsing into him made his knees weak.

No. No. No. Hell, no. He'd only felt that once before in his life and he wasn't about to do that again.

When he jumped back, she beat him to the punch line. "That is *so* not going to happen. Understood?"

He nodded, not trusting himself to speak.

"Sit, before you fall down." Her hands trembled as she snapped open the old metal first aid kit and searched the bins.

Sitting in one of two chairs, he noticed that there was two of everything. "So, you married?"

"None of your business. Close your eyes. This is going to sting." She pressed an antiseptic pad against the cut on his forehead.

"Ow. Damn. Stop that."

Without thinking, he grabbed her hand and bam. There it was again. No denying it. She was a witch, and a powerful one at that. She'd probably be a perfect match for him if he was looking for a mate. Which he damn well was not.

"Do you mind?" She stared at where he held her hand, unable to let go. Dark eyelashes framed the most stunning pale blue eyes he'd ever seen.

The warmth coursing from her essence turned his brain to mush. It nourished him, fed him, and made him whole in a way he'd never felt before. Thinking to grab anything but her, he picked up an old framed photograph of a woman and a little girl. A younger version of the badger-princess.

"Jesus. Stop touching my stuff. What's wrong with you? Give me that." She put it back, adjusting it on the shelf several times until perfect.

"Is that you?" he asked, trying hard to find conversation.

She glared and pointedly ignored him by hand-cranking an ancient generator. The World War II radio crackled and came to life.

"Jelly? Are you there? It's me, Terra." Three-inch tubes glowed as she spoke into a microphone.

"Sure am, Hun. What can I do you for?" A crackly voice spoke from an ancient speaker.

"Can you get a tow truck out to my place? Some *idiot* with an ATV got all tangled up in the gulch." Crossing her hands over her bountiful chest, she frowned in his direction.

"That's a ten-four. Anything else? Milk? Bread?"

"Nope. I'm good, thanks. K-C-B-Two-Five-Two. Out."

"W-9-Fifteen-Fifteen. Out"

Who the hell was this woman?

Her eyes blazed, and he didn't miss the distrust and small edge of fear that flickered beneath.

He cleared his throat. "Ah, maybe I'll just wait outside by my vehicle."

"Good idea." She threw him a bottle of water, nodded in the direction of the stones, and said, "Do me a favor. Don't tell anyone you saw those. I don't need people snooping around."

"You found a unique vein, didn't you?"

"You know turquoise?" She chewed on her bottom lip and her brows turned down.

"I'm known to collect a piece here and there." He studied her mouth, and his dick urged him to make a move. He shut it up quick. Not going to happen.

"I mean it." Her face flushed and she pointed a finger at his chest. "If you say a word, I will... argh... I don't know what I will do, but it will be really, really bad."

He swore he felt the ground move under his feet.

"Hang on there, honey. I didn't say I would tell anyone."

"I am not your honey." She dragged her fingers over her face and let out an audible sigh. "Just leave. Okay?"

He turned on his heel, walked back down to where he'd left his vehicle, and sat in the shade of a giant cactus.

His head was throbbing. His cock was swollen and aching. He couldn't get out of this place fast enough.

Of all the bad luck. Who would've thought he'd run into a powerful witch. During solstice. In the middle of the desert.

His body and magic responded in a way that made the hairs on the back of his neck stand on end.

Hell no.

Eight years wasn't long enough to make him forget the horrors of what could happen during the mating ritual.

His throat constricted, as it always did, when he thought of Megan and the last time he'd wanted to mate with a witch.

He placed his head in his hands and tried to block out the memories, but with no gaming tables, no cell phone apps, and no ATV, he had no place to hide from his thoughts.

She'd been eighteen, and beautiful, with everything to live for, and he'd killed her. Not a day went by where he didn't regret that night. She'd come on so strong, he'd just assumed she knew the rules. He moaned as the scene played out in front of him, both nightmare and mirage.

It was his first solstice and he was thinking with his cock. But what male witch didn't at that time of year? She was so fucking hot and he'd been drinking hard with his buddies. She said she was ready.

The magic foreplay started out a lot of fun. They threw light sexual energy at each other, but then it got serious.

He moaned, wishing he could erase the memory of her face when he'd thrown his first real blast of energy into her.

It wasn't until after the funeral he'd learned the truth. She was a half-breed, a pretender. God almighty, what was she thinking trying to mate with him? She must've known he was from one of most powerful clans in the world.

And why hadn't he seen it? He was stupid drunk. That's why. His buddies should've stopped him, but they'd been just as shit-faced.

Jace beat his forehead into his knees, forgetting about the wound. Fresh blood dripped down the side of his face.

Fucking awesome.

He stood, and rubbed the back of his stiff neck and groaned.

An odd black shard of stone glittered in the sun a few feet away. Curious, he wandered over and picked it up. The rock was hot and not just from the sun. It all but glowed in his hand and made his powers tingle. He conjured a small fireball. It flared high.

He threw the ball of energy at a cactus twenty feet away. The blast from his hand was twice the size and power as was his norm, and he wasn't even trying.

Shit. No wonder the little badger was so prickly.

He rushed over to his upside down ATV, pulled out his knapsack, and found his cell phone. No bars. That explained the short wave. Shit. This place was medieval. He couldn't wait to get on a plane and never come back.

His brother Jack would know more about what the stone was. He'd heard him talk about rare conduits that could increase a witch's power, but he'd never seen or felt one himself.

The buzz was almost addictive.

He wanted to try it out more, but he could feel the badger's eyes on him from her cave. No sense alerting her that he'd found one of her precious stones. At least not until he figured out what it was. She'd be pissed as hell to learn he knew yet another of her secrets.

Tucking the stone into his pocket, he sat back in the shadows and waited, doing his best to avoid the badger's occasional glance out the window. Then, an ancient tow truck stopped alongside his upside down ATV.

Woman-sized khaki pants with a camouflage tank jumped out of the cab. This had to be Jelly, based on the box of donuts on the passenger seat.

She frowned, sizing him up and down. "You know there's a no trespassing sign."

"So I've been told."

Big hands rested on wide hips and lips pursed. "Could get a big fine if the sheriff finds out."

"Is he going to?" He glared.

"Depends on what Terra says." Sniffing, she strode toward the house mumbling how he didn't scare her none. That's when he noticed the SAT phone swinging from her cracked leather belt.

Halleluiah. "Wait. Can I borrow your phone?"

She turned and grinned. "Sure. It'll cost you. Sat-phones ain't cheap."

"Tack it onto the cost of my tow."

"That'll work just fine. Can I see your card?" Her palm shot out as he dug his wallet out of his dusty jeans. He handed her his Amex.

With her nose to the plastic, she read, "F-i-a-l-k-o…Like the New York Fialko's in the news?"

"No relation," he lied. The last thing he needed was someone knowing his brother was a b'zillionaire.

She slid the card through an ancient mechanical device and handed him back his card. "I'll be right back. Don't go anywhere."

"Where the hell would I go?" Grumbling, he picked up the satellite phone and dialed his brother. "Hey, Jack."

"I thought you were off the grid for a few days of R&R."

"Me too." He raked his fingers through his hair, stared at his wreck, and paced. "Something came up. I was on my ATV in the middle of the desert and found a piece of what looks like black turquoise. And damned if it isn't hot to the touch. It's got some kind of magical properties. Possibly a conduit of sorts."

"Hold on while I login to our site. Takes a few minutes. The guys in IT have it so secure that even I can't get in without an act of God." After a long silence and much clicking of a keyboard, Jack let out a long whistle. "Call me back when you find a land line. Use the encrypted number."

Jace scratched the back of his neck and kicked the dirt with the toe of his boot. Figures the woman was hiding something big. Fuck. He should hop on the next plane out of there and let his brother deal with this shit. Jack was the expert. Plus the man was already mated, so there was no danger of the little badger working her solstice magic on him.

"Everything else okay?" Jack asked.

Hell no. But he couldn't let his big brother know how the little badger had affected him. Jack would be up in his face about it, his mother and sister would come, and they'd have him in a wedding tux by week's end. He'd just not touch the witch again. Once solstice was over, the mating urge would subside, and he could get on with his life.

"Nah, I'm good. Call you back in an hour or so."

They said their goodbyes.

Five days of solstice hell left to go. His cock swelled, thinking about her naked under him.

Shut up dick-head. We're not mating. We'll find a willing, sweet thing in Vegas, pick her up, and have meaningless sex.

His cock disagreed.

Read more:
https://www.amazon.com/Dark-Tremor-Mated-Magic-Book-ebook/dp/B01DWIXD0K

Free on Kindle Unlimited

About the Authors

Stella Marie Alden loves Zumba, yoga, watercolor painting, and fixing up her house. Growing up in Vermont, she loved to make up stories. Crayons fought each other over size and placement in their cardboard box and imaginary friends crowded the house. Her brother often complained. "Tell her no one's here, Mother."
Her career paths have varied. She's been a librarian, a classical clarinetist, recording studio engineer, broadcast electronics repairman, and now she architects software programs. She lives in Bergen County, NJ with her lifelong hero and their two cats.
www.stellamariealden.com

Chantel Seabrook is the author of the Amazon bestselling fantasy romance Cara's Twelve, as well as the Therian Agents paranormal romance series, and co-author of the Mated by Magic series.

When she isn't reading or writing sexy stories, she's most likely spending time with her family, cooking, singing, or racing between soccer, hockey and karate practices. She's living her own happily ever after with her husband of fifteen years and their two daughters.

She loves creating new exciting characters - from sexy, bad boy alphas, to the passionate, fiery women who love them.

Canadian born and bred, she started life in Edmonton, Alberta, and now resides in London, Ontario. She attended Western University where she graduated with an Honors degree in Anthropology.

Her guilty pleasures include red wine, pasta, binge watching Starz originals, and hanging out with her rescue pup, Jaxx.

She loves to hear from her readers and can be reached at chantelseabrook@gmail.com